Mechanisms of Loss

Mechanisms of Loss

TWO NOVELLAS

MICHEL FAÏS

TRANSLATED FROM THE GREEK

BY DAVID CONNOLLY

FOREWORD BY KATERINA SCHINA

AFTERWORD BY VANGELIS HATZIVASILEIOU

YALE UNIVERSITY PRESS ■ NEW HAVEN & LONDON

A MARGELLOS
WORLD REPUBLIC OF LETTERS BOOK

English translation copyright © 2021 by David Connolly.
Aegypius monachus was originally published in Greek in 2001. A revised edition, from which this translation was made, was originally published in Greek by Patakis Publishers, © S. Patakis S.A. & Michel Faïs, Athens 2013. *Lady Cortisol* was originally published in Greek by Patakis Publishers, © S. Patakis S.A. & Michel Faïs, Athens 2016.

Yale University Press books may be purchased in quantity for educational, business, or promotional use. For information, please e-mail sales.press@yale.edu (U.S. office) or sales@yaleup.co.uk (U.K. office).

Set in Electra and Nobel type by Tseng Information Systems, Inc.
Printed in the United States of America.

Library of Congress Control Number: 2020933180
ISBN 978-0-300-23717-7 (hardcover : alk. paper)

A catalogue record for this book is available from the British Library.

This paper meets the requirements of ANSI/NISO z39.48-1992 (Permanence of Paper).

10 9 8 7 6 5 4 3 2 1

CONTENTS

FOREWORD

What is it about Michel Faïs's prose that so unsettles the reader? The narrator's constant contention with himself? The frenetic submersion into an inner world? The vulgar dissection of the self? The daring with which this self opens up to the other? The despair of the bereaved who embodies, idealizes, shatters, restructures, butchers, and devours the object lost? The constant raking of grief's subsoil so that, by the same action, the author might dispel its torment? The thrill of a sexual struggle with no limits? The rejection of temporal succession and spatial delimitation? The complete interchangeability of the base and the sublime? Or is it perhaps, in the end, the poetry of his rampaging prose, the music imbuing his diction — the staccato giving the reader the impression that a metronome is ticking imperiously within the text — or the gasping rhythm of his score?

In Faïs's often broken, fragmented, galloping discourse, one discerns an author who employs the concepts of spoken, prepositional language as if they were the concepts of music, parables broken off in mid-sentence. If his prose resembles music, it is because, just as happens with music, what he has to say is revealed and at the same time concealed — and I am referring here mainly to his works that express an autobiographical angst. Just as every piece of music points to something beyond itself, functioning as a spark of revocation or reaction ushering us into a dream or a nightmare, so, too, Faïs's prose displays an anguished attempt to name things, not to convey concepts.

In *Lady Cortisol*, which is an endless question-and-answer session between a man who is asking and a woman who is answering, an unspecified narrator keeps intervening, like a drummer giving the tone and rhythm on an unpredictable voyage in stormy waters. In the autobiographical novella *Aegypius monachus*, a feverish text that explodes narrative techniques by parodying them, there is the ceaseless working of the cogs of an inexorable machine that grinds time, animating dead objects with sounds that belong to the past. The basis, however, of the rhythmic mode in Faïs's works is disturbed. Halting, sudden spurts, panting, silences, the white noise of the unconscious; words left suspended, contracted sentences, an incessant prattle that often flows into the comical, bold descriptions that verge on the surrealistic; unbridled, overlapping voices that produce a peculiar cacophony, an anguished sound structure of whispers, cries, murmurings, a serial composition that never arrives at the comforting solution of tonality. From the tramping of the sentence to the lethargic drowsiness of words emptied of their meaning, this seemingly undisciplined but actually completely controlled prose condenses the anguished and ineffectual attempt of the subject narrated to give form to the formless, a foundation to the mercurial, to reconstruct the tatters of the self through its free associations, sudden recollections, details arriving unexpectedly, vacillations, vicissitudes, contradictions. Yet all it succeeds in doing is writhe, surrendered to the tatters of nothingness.

Faïs stretches language to its limits in order to penetrate the unchartered, chaotic realm of existential angst. In his writing we at times encounter the percussive use of disagreement and a resounding dynamic, and at others a hypnotic repetition of common motifs—that is to say, of writing obsessions. If I were to attempt in one word to express the stylistic order of Faïs's writing, I might speak of variation (borrowing the term from music): a variation in the sense of a constant divergence and prose disorder, allowing his themes (memory, grief, trauma, fantasy, loss) to emerge one from the other and to vanish one into the other. They briefly appear held motionless on the agitated surface of his language before sinking into the ineffable.

Theodor Adorno saw music as an odyssey of endless mediation in order to capture the impossible. Just such an odyssey is that undertaken by the language of Michel Faïs, even if it be a loss, as the author well knows, even if it cannot possibly grasp the thing. For it is equally impossible for it, animated as it is by its own weakness, not to be ceaselessly magnetized by all it has experienced but never subjugated, by all that will forever remain out of range, perpetually evasive, yet always there to be hunted. And it is then that it discharges into music, just as the reflexive language of *Aegypius monachus* ends in music on the last page of this constantly self-undermining yet ever surviving remarkable book.

Katerina Schina

Mechanisms of Loss

Aegypius monachus

What is to burn is as if already burned. — Talmud

Eventually you break with the past. You have to, you grow tired, take to your heels. All change. Remember the conductors of old? All chaaange. Part cantors, part market sellers. All chaaange. Your father again and again phoning his relatives drowned in the Danube. All chaaange. Your mother shouting, *I'm on my own, I'm not on the bottle*. All chaaange. The circus of family suffering eventually packs up and moves on. All chaaange. Then you become your father's father and, taking an ax, smash the telephone; then you become your mother's mother and start slapping her around till you bloody her lips. No, all this takes place in another life, and you've not snuffed it yet to know what goes on in the sky's underground tunnels. You don't become anything. The most exciting thing that can happen to you is to hold on to the rings for the "ducks" you didn't hit, the ticket for the ghost train you didn't validate, the gifts in the shooting gallery you didn't win. Not even that. Memories of an age when memories shot up like dandelions, you say to yourself, to that screwed-up old pal of yours. *Eventually, you break with the past.* Not a word. *You have to, you grow tired, take to your heels. All chaaange.* He flauntingly turns his back. In body slang that means it's time for a fairy tale.

Once upon a time, there lived a family in a town up to the knees in mud, a hollow with low-roofed houses, where you couldn't see a hand in front of you because of the thick mist, where only heaven could help you if you got lost in its narrow lanes. It was in this town, then, amid the clackety-clack, clackety-clack, clackety-clack, that a boy was born with freckles, goggling eyes, and legs like straws. Seeing his father pondering complex chess problems while his mother was avidly gazing at travel guides, the boy acquired a melancholic bent. Which is why from an early age, he showed a remarkable aptitude for lies and secrets. The first lie he came up with was that he couldn't speak normally. For twenty-five years, no less, there were those who felt pity and those who made fun of the boy from the muddy city who mumbled his words as if he had a mouth full of current cake with chocolate filling. And so he never, but never, went unnoticed. For his parents, his teachers, his friends, and the young girls, he was someone to be singled out, either as a poor wretch or as a p-p-poor wretch. Nevertheless, this boy from the slithery town may have needed a full half-day to finish a sentence when in front of people, yet when he sang, when he mumbled in his sleep, and when, shut up in his room, he read aloud, what seashells she sells on the seashore and what pecks of pickled peppers Peter Piper picked! And I ask you, straight up, is there any secret more terrible than that? From the moment, that is, that someone refuses to speak in song, to speak clearly as in his dreams and shuts himself in his room acting the orator, well I'm sorry, he deserves to boil in his own juice like a crab.

Even when all his teeth have fallen out and he's unable to put one foot in front of the other this fairy tale will continue to lull him to sleep. There, he's already snoring. Is he grinding his teeth yet? A sign that the level of his lyricism has reached the danger point. From now on, if you so much as think of giving a kick to make the first years of his youth come back, he'll begin grunting. At least now your mind is at rest. Is it nighttime? Daytime? Is it nighttime that's stuffed itself with pills and can't open its eyelids? Is it daytime that feels paralyzed at the idea of darkness and brazenly dawdles? The one sure thing is the fart he lets out. Has he turned on his stomach? Oh, here we go again with a family drama. It's a mathematical certainty. The moment he adopts the position of the cowardly slain, he sees his parents sitting at the table and worrying themselves sick. Does he have his head in his hands too? The questions begin. Daddy, were Michel, Clara, Daisy, Isaac, Simandof, and Granny Rivka shot in the head before being thrown into the Danube? Mommy, when was the last time you lay down naked with Daddy? Mommy and Daddy, before I started to stutter, did I speak properly like everyone else? Listen, Son, before they threw your uncle, your aunt, your three cousins, and your grandma into the waters of the Danube, they roasted them in kosher lard. Your mommy had you with the milkman, the mailman, the greengrocer, the butcher, and the man at the corner shop. Before you began stuttering, you were a deaf-mute. Just for one day, make me your progenitors, just one day. You'll see your pride and joy, and you'll have to rub your little eyes. He's turned on his back. When awake everything may be a mess, when asleep, though, everything gets worked out. Face down, family matters, face up, everything sexual, sideways, the rest. His eyelids are flickering. He's probably dreaming. His underpants aren't bulging, anyway. So he's dreaming that he's falling into bed with the woman he betrayed, with the woman who saved him from himself, with the woman he ill-treated for years with the violence of

7

the impotent. Dearest, what a torment! Not to be able to get it up with the only woman who managed to break through your blocked-up breast while you get a bad case of priapism for whatever floozy appears before you. He opens his eyes. Surprisingly, he gets up in a good mood. In fine fettle. As if it were his shift in the creation of the world. While drinking his cup of tea, he'll make his plans for survival. Following a separation, you mustn't forget, you must remember. Left right, left right. How did you sleep, how did you eat, how did you breathe? On the spot, 'tention. A-a-at ease. Don't get dizzy from the intoxication of forgetting: burn the photos, paint the house, break with common friends. Get in line, Rookie. No sinking, no celebration, concentration. Damn and blast you. A hundred squats fully equipped. Rally around yourself. Meaning? Tap-tap the head, tick-tock the heart, ooh-ooh the goolies. Before long he gives up on teach yourself philosophy and takes up grocery-store mathematics. So what do we have then? One kilo of suffocating familiarity and one kilo of lusting loneliness add up to a life condemned to *in all likelihood*. He tightens his belt with pride. He, at least, went against the current. He didn't submit to the modern thinking that requires you to have your cake and eat it. You're a shit-heap of lies. It's me you're talking to, all right? Don't get me started. Whether you screw around with your eyes or with your dick, it's all the same. That's the first thing. We leave someone when we use the bed only for flaking out and the table only for stuffing our bellies. That's the second thing. Whether you're a surgeon or a butcher, you get your hands dirty when you start cutting. As for the third, do you want me to spell it out for you? Have you seen how the little jerk whistles in the elevator? In the trolley, on his way to the publisher, he jots down in his notepad a phrase filched from the lips of a passenger. A story in the making? Encouragement from a stranger? Neither a story nor encouragement. The time of the literary grudge has long passed. What did you think? That with paper and pencil we can carpet all those who've led us to the point of walking around as doubles of our own selves? The time of trusting foreigners is long passed. How long are we going to go on giving solace to the suburban grief of the man next door? How long are we going to go on tolerating the cosmopolitan ennui of the man who *saw the cities of many peoples and learned their ways?* An incurable perversion of remembering. Just that. A Japanese when it comes to a diary. At most. A seductive voice: write, write, write. The same one always. Lifeless yet domineering. The same little voice that sewed up his mouth during the years of imposed silence now grabs his hand with the pencil. At least when he's sketching words, movements, looks, he's not splitting whatever hairs of the moment. Is it me who, on my way to the publishers, jots down in my notepad a phrase from some passerby that I'm never going to see again? Is it me who utters a sentence and someone else, who, crossing my path, jots down something hurriedly and disappears? Am I a duplicate who goes to his publishers and at the same time doesn't know where he's going? Who records in his notebook whatever he says to himself at the very same moment? Or perhaps I'm just a nobody? Since at the same time I'm watching someone speaking and someone pinching the phrase from his lips, while simultaneously I have the impression that I'm watching the phantom of someone with his lips sealed and of someone with his hands in his pockets. That's why I'm telling you, a story dragged by the hair, a plot saved from the precipice. I'll lose my mind with it. A beginning, I was born on April Fool's Day. An end, amen. A middle, I haven't traveled, have no children, don't speak any other languages, I devoted myself however to masturbation and ping-pong, worshipped frozen yogurt, *thé fumé,* and the voice of Oum Kalsoum. Get a move on, anything at all, we're in a rush. Can't you see? Words for the scrap heap. Something that doesn't recall a yawn, a gasp, a groan. Lend a hand to put an end to this hubbub of silence that's his mind. Just between us, I can no longer control him. He can only be restrained with difficulty. The hour is nigh when he'll rush out into the streets like the madman with the ax. And whoever refuses to tell his life story before him, crying for help, he'll cut to pieces. And don't let it enter your little heads that you can get away with an onrush of words that don't make a story. What we have is a master of the art of listening. He can even hear a pin dropping. Understand, an old hand. From the time when he blamed everything on being tongue-tied. When he wore the mask of the silent martyr in his tear-jerker comedy. And it wasn't as if I didn't give him a hint. You'll long for the time of the cankered speech, of the insurmountable labial and dental consonants, of the short breaths. And him without so much as an inkling, nothing. Agreed, friends lower their heads, girls turn tail, strangers see you as a joke. But just consider: is it the defect that produces the character or the character the defect? Eventually the cup turns over without the wine being spilled. And then you're all at sea. And him without so much as an inkling. From the foundations. Demolition. Any old iron? Old prayers, old hugs, old tears, old questions, old furniture. And with these sad recapitulations, he goes into the restaurant and orders lentil soup. I've seen it time and time again: when he's downhearted, he takes refuge in the pottage of Jacob and Esau. Perhaps the iron acts on his organism as an antidepressant? Anyhow, after he separated, for months his diet included nothing but the *restorative, papilionaceous, dicotyledonous legume;* lentils, salted tunny, and village bread. 'Cause he's house-proud. Come day, go day, the pot's hissing and the pan's sizzling. His bachelor life had nothing to do with burnt eggs or soggy pasta or cold kebabs from the neighborhood takeout. He may talk to the walls, but the place of eating remains sacred. Breakfast, lunch, and dinner may very well be served with a heavy heart, but never hurriedly or scrappily. I sit facing him. A grouch, he pushes the spoon into his mouth as if he were feeding an old man who shits himself. A photo from the future obliges him to eat with a little more zeal. He's surrounded by sleepy eyes, callused hands, swollen feet. A paid, multinational family. Albanian women clean for him, Romanian women iron his clothes, while Filipino women take him for a walk, Pakistani women wash and change him. All of them — mother, father, wife, sister, children, grandchildren. On the way home, he halts. Two old men on a park bench are talking. They'd sit with a few olives and nuts, says the bashful one. Where did he put so much wine? Didn't he have a belly? Didn't he have any insides? says the beaming one. They never had any problems or stress, says the bashful one. He was like a rake. Nephew, he said to me, when I sober up, I'll go on a binge, says the beaming one. And they drank. Not like today, with an eye on the clock, says the bashful one. Always under the influence, my old uncle, do you remember him? says the beaming one. As if I could forget, says the bashful one. When I'm out of sorts, I want to laugh all the time, my old uncle used to say, says the beaming one. Good years, says the bashful one. He'd be sitting under the mulberry . . . , says the beaming one. I can see him now, says the bashful one. He'd stick glass in the ground so they wouldn't steal his berries, says the beaming one. And in the tree, says the bashful one. You little devil, why do you steal them? They're yours. The berries and the tree and that ruin of a house and the demon you've got inside you. That's what he'd say to me, says the beaming one. How it sparkled after the rain . . . , says the bashful one. The mulberry? says the beaming one. The glass, what mulberry? says the bashful one. Blackberries, juicy ones, says the beaming one. Well, not black ones, says the bashful one. Not black what? says the beaming one. Berries, says the bashful one. What do you mean? says the beaming one. What I said, says the bashful one. All right, they were loquats, says the beaming one. Loquats they may have been, but they weren't black, says the bashful one. Have you forgotten what our faces looked like, as if they'd been smeared with soot? says the beaming one. From the blackberries? says the bashful one. No, from the white ones, says the beaming one. Do you remember Marios? says the bashful one. What's Marios got to do with the berries? says the beaming one. Do you remember him or not? says the bashful one. Better than you, says the beaming one. Do you remember what work he did? says the bashful one. You're asking me if I know what work Marios did? says the beaming one. You tell me, says the bashful one. I don't know, you tell me, says the bashful one. Well, during the December Uprising, my ol' uncle hid Marios in his house, says the beaming one. So what? says the bashful one. And you sit there and ask me what work he did? says the beaming one. Yes, I'm asking you. Is it forbidden? says the bashful one. Yes it's forbidden, says the beaming one. He was a coalman. Got it? says the bashful one. Because I told you he was an ice cream man, says the beaming one. He sold coal. And our faces were black because we used to play in the coal yard. Co-oal. And the blackberries were as white as snow. Coal. As for your uncle, he was an old shitbag, a lousy collaborator. And who'd be hiding who? Wasn't Marios a killer, armed? says the bashful one, now looking up. And the beaming one, now pale as wax, droops and simply sighs. All right. It's not the best possible dialogue. There were times when he'd stumble over even more casual conversations. Fragments of life gave him a friendly pat on the shoulders, fragments of life shook his hand, fragments of life turned him back. To former years. When people laughed at nothing, cried at nothing, felt replete with nothing, amused themselves with nothing, believed in nothing, died for nothing. Tales of a former age. When everybody emerged from something big. Pain, secret, lie— narration, in other words. Then, even a fall wasn't just everyone's affair. Because the thud made by the body and the plop made by the soul concerned the person next to you, and it concerned him because, quite simply, you fell together. But whatever the case, better for him to meet people who quarrel with one another than people who keep silent. For him to have something in order to forget. Like the wretched old man who has the transistor glued to his ear all day long, like the cantankerous fellow who quarrels with himself, like the kid who plays on his own and mixes up the subjects. Anyhow. With one thing and another he arrives home. During the half-hour that he gets some shut-eye, he dreams that someone creeps up like a cat, lies down naked beside him. How will he be in thirty years' time? Someone who once looked like two drops of water, an old lecher now, with a pitted face, wrinkled hands yet lusty flesh. Someone whose only concern is to mate with his soul, lies down on his bed. He curls up beside him and, as if murmuring obscenities in his ear, begins to remind him of whatever sordid act he'd committed, whatever sordid act he'd not committed but had contemplated so thoroughly that it was as if he had committed it.

The complete works of one ill-fated. The deeply buried cassette of his life. Played again and again. You're one of those from Turkish parts, you're neither a Jew nor a Christian, all you know is how to walk the streets. In all weathers, outside. Have you got hemorrhoids? But because you're a big fart, the television on, the tea tepid, the slippers level with the armchair. Whatever time you come home. Whatever shit they serve you with. Whatever little devil you take a shine to. Our stay-at-home self at the ready. As for the rest, the half-learning of romanticism. You'll return home arm in arm with the woman you'll live with for the rest of your life, in your head you'll write the book that will redeem you from writing, you'll meet the parents who will bring you up again from the beginning. Can't you keep still, you know, when Halima shuts up, Joan of Arc begins grousing. That's the direction you're going in. And doing a ton. I rest my forehead on his pillow. He wakes up with a start. In order to break free of the image of his dirty old self, he unbuttons his pajama trousers, thrusting his hand between his legs. It's impossible for him to concentrate. Once he was absorbed by his mother. That is, by her breast that he didn't suckle, by her bulging eyes when she was annoyed, by her fingers yellowed from the nicotine, and, without question, by her ragged heels that she tried to restore with pumice stone and lukewarm saline foot solution; but above all by her lascivious kisses, these above all, kisses that mother and son exchanged in their sleep, without arms and legs, with strange skin diseases on the face, as they rolled, locked by their lips, funny, horrid little balls. Now, the lifelong beloved. Now she puts wedding rings of spunk on all the fingers of his trembling hand, of the spunk that became an ax and cut them to pieces when it stopped flowing between them. Which is why asses, cunts, armpits, thighs, and tits vanish like summer clouds the moment he hears her hoarse laughter, the moment he confronts her misty slant eyes, the moment he smells the milk of her skin. The asses, cunts, armpits, thighs, and tits that aren't hers. As hers have become fresh-smelling bedsheets, well-laid tables, wintry Saturday nights with a checked blanket in front of the television, holidays with laughter to the point of tears, a daily life that seized something from the sweetness of eternity. And then, deterministically, the asses, cunts, armpits, thighs, and tits that aren't hers became heated quarrels, threats, and oaths, retrogressions, divisions, decisions, and, in between, ruthless word games, last words, that are never the last ones. The asses, cunts, thighs, armpits, and tits that don't belong to any woman, given that they're not parts of the human body but flayed living thoughts that guide him, decayed dreams that pad his life, horrifying memories that suckle his present. He sits at his desk. Swivels in his ergonomic chair. Stares at his sharpened pencils, his different-colored pens, the erasers and pencil sharpeners all lined up. Everything's gone before. Forget it. Scritz scratz, scritz scratz, scritz scratz, the pencil over the paper. Tap-tap-tap-dring, tap-tap-tap-dring, tap-tap-tap-dring, the fingers on the typewriter. There was a time when he'd get out of bed with the nightmare of the blank page and get into bed with the nightmare of the one filled, crumpled, stuffed with a reality that was unable to move aside so as to give a little space to the reality of someone else, to clear its head, its heart and the rancor of its own reality so as to feel the reality of the other, the stranger, the passerby. The one he looks at but doesn't see. The one he wants to slap, to erase from the face of the earth, to bend down and suck off, to hold forever in his arms, to stare in the eye like a lame dog. Which is why after all he wears out his shoes on the god-awful streets of a town that's not for walking by any means. In order to tire his reality. To curb its ravings, its panic, its hard-on, its guffawing. Which is why, of course, whatever half-baked, acceptable piece of shit he's scribbled, he's done it by getting away from the incessant dawdling of existence—that constant worktime with the ego, that gibber-gibber with zilch that goes on without end. He turns off the light and lies down on the sofa. Without sleeping, without not sleeping. Lying there, he watches himself opening the door while he's lying down with that hovering feeling of lethargy, going down in the elevator while he's lying down with that hovering feeling of lethargy, taking hold of the chrome handle on the passenger door of the seven-seater black taxi while he's lying down with that hovering feeling of lethargy, sitting in the front seat of the taxi from his childhood, from his writing and his successive dreams while he's lying down with that hovering feeling of lethargy, arriving at the "city of old, demolished in years long passed" with the astral speed of desire with no return.

There, he begins rolling in the mud of Boukloutzas, counting the buttons in tiny Jewish shops, gazing at the snow in the prewar photos by Papazekos, throwing confetti over the remarried wife of Vizyinos's younger brother, looking at Makis approaching on his bicycle, listening to flutes, bagpipes, and drums, smelling burnt wood after a rainfall, eating roasted offal from Aunt Clara's widestretched legs, warming his own numbed hands in Melaniasmeni's blue hands, disappearing inside bordellos, swallowing grout in the company of the blue-eyed gravedigger, and.

Enough, he tells me.

All right, but only for today, I reply.

Of course, his *enough* means don't stop, don't stop talking to me even for a moment. Talk to me, why are you sitting there and staring at me? Talk to me, what am I saying, you will talk, you'll talk to me till the next life. Even if you keep on repeating to him like a parrot, *I've nothing else to say,* till his nerves are in shreds, he still prefers that to a dumb silence. Of course, saying he prefers it is a figure of speech. Given that there's no question of choice but rather of immediate priority. Because you too, you'd have the same reaction if every time you lacked a human voice to keep you company your head was filled with a band of deaf musicians playing tunes, waltzes, bossa novas and rebetika rhythms that took you back to the old haunts of shame, boredom, and fear of shame and boredom. So you can guess just what kind of present day is his present day.

Where were we up to? he asks. Where were we up to, where were we up to. We were up to where we *were up to,* I tell him. We were? We were up to, up to the blue-eyed gravedigger, I tell him. He lights a cigarette. When he doesn't have anything to say, he lights a cigarette. In the way that someone else lets out an *Oh Christ* into empty space or sighs inside, *boy oh boy.* He begins puffing away.

He switches on the television. A white-covered mountain appears. The lens guides us round a ghost village. Two inhabitants. Cut off for six months. A record for solitude, says the presenter with buttonhole eyes. An old man emerges from a stable, and an old woman is carrying two logs. In Snowton, the presenter with the buttonhole eyes continues, the winter never ends. Our friend begins to snivel as he watches the old man and woman laughing like little children. I have the sheep. The woman has three goats. In the house, the stove's roaring. That's life, says the old man. That's your life, you stupid jerk, he shouts at him. Who are you to tell me that's life. Stupid jerk, he goes on till the cigarette end burns his fingers.

The truth is that small communities cause him consternation. Places where one person says good morning to another cause him to panic. Houses built side by side, frightened children, intoxicated by high spirits, lined up for shooting, choke him; the houses where the neighbor's dream gets under the quilt and passes into your dream, like a fart, a disease, an evil spirit, and whatever else your mind can come up with. For, he reflects, to eat bean soup and dream that you're eating suckling pig is no big deal. But to see in your sleep that you go to bed with your wife and in the morning find yourself hugging your dead neighbor? That's why all those who nail horseshoes, weave baskets, milk animals, plow the land till they peg out, interposing lullabies, wedding marches, and funeral dirges between their bodies and time, call him to account.

What are you thinking at this moment? This unmoving life is submitting him to bastinado, shoving boiling hot eggs into his armpits, torturing him through insomnia. Just like the countryside. Pure, simple nature so beloved of hermits, lovers, landscape painters, photographers, suicides. What are you thinking at this moment? He stumbles over a stone. What are you thinking at this moment? He breaks a twig. What are you thinking at this moment?

He turns off the television and goes into the kitchen. He eats a croissant and drinks a mouthful of Coca-Cola. He belches. A home, a book, a wife, he says through his teeth. He farts. When you talk, you say less, he continues, admonishing himself. Because I know what a joker he is, he'll put aside the big words before long and set memory's chainsaw in motion.

I'd like to be with somebody like you but not with you. Those are the words she's been trying to tell him for a long time now. For years, she's been preparing herself for this moment. She's got them on the tip of her tongue, and yet, when she opens her mouth, she's like a mute. She's got them on the tip of her pen, yet, when she sits down to write them, it's the arm of an illiterate that hangs from her shoulder.

Twelve words. Twenty-four consonants. Eighteen vowels. She won't say those words. She'll roll them like lava in her mouth. Never. She'll swallow them like the drowning do water. Never to him. Even if she lives to be as old as Sarah. Never to him who was her lost family. Her lips won't formulate those words. Never to him who was her re-found sleep, her re-found hunger, the re-found stories of her life. Not even over his grave. And that's the end of it.

Will she just think them? Yes. Will she wake up yelling them in the most inaccessible nooks of her sleep? Yes. Will she whisper them to passing men who have something of his gaze, his voice, his gait? Yes. When he's out of the house, will she wear his jacket, will she wear his shoes, will she sit in his chair, and, gazing at her photo on his desk, will she repeat them like a prayer, like a punishment, like some kind of onanism? Yes. Yes. Yes. At the moment that their two bodies part in bed, will she say them to him distorted between words taken from her breast or from her loins? No. Why? Later comes the *yes* and the *no*. First the story.

Her childhood was a tree in the center of a huge open space. A dry piece of wood stuck in a vacant lot where everyone threw out the garbage. She was the only one who didn't disregard that tree, which might have been taken for anything but a tree. After school she'd run with longing and hug it tightly. Then she'd squeeze into its hollow and imagine that outside the world had ended. She couldn't hear even the car horns, or the sea breeze, or the other children's voices. Just before leaving her refuge, she'd decorate it with gum, chocolate, barrettes, bows, pencils, pencil sharpeners, dollies. These gifts were her small atonement for her big forbidden wishes. What did she want? Why, that one of them should die. Naturally, she trembled afterward on her pillow as if she had a fever coming on. For, if her mother were to die, her father would turn the whole house into a mausoleum and, like a true Cerberus outside the dead woman's room, wouldn't allow so much as a mosquito to disturb her rest. Whereas, if her father were to die, her mother would call the ragman to come and take everything, including the walls from the man's room. Then she'd put in her earplugs, wear her dark glasses, and never get out of bed again. While she, young, middle-aged, old, would tear herself apart in order to support her guardian father and her bedridden mother. How fortunate it is that childhood wishes never come true. Since, as with all children, their twisted attempt to create midget adults and giant objects shines like a candle in a hollowed gourd.

Our love life is our family life. No lullaby, no caress, no game, no burning, no mirror deeper than blood. Just as the men she loved and ceased to love whirl in her memory, so in the same way her father and mother whirl in a dance that they never danced together. And just as the caresses of men she left and who left her peel away from her skin, so in the same way her parents peel away like plaster from the ceiling. Which is why she entreated like her father, when her mother would be on the doorstep with bags in hand at the slightest thing, and at other times her mind would cloud at her mother's paranoid laughter when, like a little boy, her father would run after her to satisfy her outrageous demands. Since her mother never left home for good and her father never begged for her attention to the point that she totally loathed him. Which is why she too desired men in the manner of nonseparation and non-loathing. And just as her father knew only too well that the more blindly he offered his wife everything, the more he bound her to him, so she surrendered herself to men in the cunning manner of the master bound by the servant.

For with the men she went with from time to time, the sapphire gleam of her knees, especially the beautiful brown nape of her neck, the nipples of course how they shine in the dark, without doubt the funny knees, and those feet, which like bows stretched passion tight — agreed, agreed — but, more than anything, her every entanglement showed that she'd remain married to the grave with him who, *I love your mother more than my own life, more than even you, dear,* and with her who, *from the time you were born, your father has never again seen my naked body.*

■ ■ ■

There are times when she closes her eyes and sees him suddenly driving her out, for good, without cause, or finds him in bed with her best friend, going out for a moment for cigarettes and then vanishing, or reading in his diary the most horrible thoughts concerning their daily lives.

At least when they leave you, no matter how they leave you, you have to deal with something. Your egoism, your sorrow, your loneliness. But what about when you're with someone, and the aim of your life, a noose round your neck, a hook in your insides, an anvil tied to your feet, is nonseparation tossed in an ocean of separation?

Which is why the moment she opens her eyes she sees again and again something she's seen before again and again. She's in the dining room, the bedroom, the backyard, in that distant point of memory, the most silent, the most untouched, the most primitive. There where nothing leaves anything else. There where everything is condemned to the most vulgar proximity, subject to the most pilloried snugness, when suddenly the father and mother grab hold of the chairs, the bed, the table, the fig tree, even the roses, in their attempt to save whatever they can from a whirlwind that comes from no one knows where. Because outside the sun's shining, bliss as they say, and, without a care, they're drinking their cherry juice, listening to sentimental songs on the radio, till they hear that whoooosh. A terrifying noise that's about to uproot everything, to swallow their lives; a whoooosh that no one knows whether it's in their heads or if it really is some form of tropical phenomenon that, totally incomprehensibly, is knocking at the door.

She's not going to leave him; the idea of separation is not going to leave her. Of course, this diptych doesn't mean reconciliation with decay. Eventually, everything comes to an end, expires, so it's better that it fade alongside tried and tested familiarity. That rejection of separation, with separation having bitten hold of separation between the eyes, means that you don't have the right to separate; you're deprived of that right. It means that you're regarded as an immigrant in the land of Separation. You roam in a land where you don't know a word of the language, you feed yourself on garbage, sleep on benches, and if they catch you, you're in big trouble; without your realizing it, they'll send you back to your own country. And deportation to the land of Nonseparation means that the head lowered, the entreaty, the making out that you don't understand, the father's silent arrangement and the unyielding gaze, the cheek, the rubbing of salt into the wounds and moving on, together with the mother's shrieking keep their hold in all degrees of administration, of economy, of ways of thinking. Which is why the citizens of this country don't know how to behave and are permanently with one foot in prison and the other in the madhouse.

There, today, for example, completely unexpectedly, the woman help she has in the house, while ironing, as if mumbling a dirge from her own village, said to her, *We don't cook just to eat. We don't wash just so as not to smell. We don't walk just to get somewhere. We don't put our arms around him just to show him love. That's why you're never happy, Ma'am.* Another incident. Three days ago, just as the man in the corner shop was giving her the change, he leaned over and said to her, *You can stop acting the nice, kind woman to me. You're a monster. Two-faced, through and through. All of us around here know what you are. I feel sorry for your husband. You'll suck his blood dry.* A month later, the same day, the same time, the Gypsy woman who stands outside the supermarket with her hand outstretched said to her, *Your heart's not throbbing for your husband. Your own body despises you, dearie.* And that nonstop round of self-appointed squealers concerning her inner life, a life without end, eventually shines the lamp in her face. Then she doesn't dare stare straight back at some passing man who smiles at her. Why? Because if she were to do so, at the same moment she'd spew out truths that cut her up. *You see, our love life is confined to long massages. Not very often, during the night, half-asleep, my husband and I stick our heads between each other's legs. And we stay like that. Frozen. Till daylight comes. Frozen.*

Things like that happen to her, and then she thinks she's sleepwalking or losing her wits. She hears them talking about her behind her back, and she thinks she's become a topic of conversation among people who have no right. Yet they take it upon themselves, become provocative, interfere in her thoughts, determine her movements, dictate her wishes. Given that all of them are most likely people who iron for her, supply her with her cigarettes, ask her for charity, they pass her by indifferently; actually, though, they're temptations, temptations that prevent her from breaking free of the experience of separation. And instead of wearing a necklace of garlic, spitting three times in her breast, taking a thick straw broom and chasing all those wretched demons out of her house, out of her heart, she stands there and starts up a conversation with them.

Afterward, it's no surprise, is it, that she views happiness as a carnival of unhappiness?

■ ■ ■

Agreed. They decided not to have children. And because of that decision, they were regarded as being self-centered (by their enemies), devoted to their work (by their friends), totally in love (by their own folks). The truth revealed itself to no one. The truth is concealed behind words. Words save us from truth. When we have the words for a thing, when we feel that we describe something exactly, we feel, at the same time, that the thing itself kicks us away, that it expels us from its meaning, that it abandons us in its own empty representation. In a strange sort of way, at the same time, the thing becomes the kick, the expelled meaning, its embalmed image. Even more so when that same thing, the thing you're called upon to describe, is like resignation in flight, consumption in fear, devotion in panic.

With one thing and another, the merciless god of asphyxiation came and installed himself in their home. He ate from their plate, slept in their bed, chatted with them like an old and trusted friend. So even the last sad specter of desire left them. On precisely that day, which is not sufficiently day; a day, however, sated with night, a day that you never want to see the likes of again but that doesn't do you that favor, of course, since every day from now on, better never to start, is that same identical day dawning; on that day then, a day sated with night and refusing to dawn, she began keeping all-night vigil for him as if for the dead. What did she do exactly? She'd pretend to be asleep and as soon as he'd closed his eyes, she'd get up, remain still till her eyes were accustomed to the darkness and stare at him. His tranquil body in the half-lit bed. Then she'd begin to weep for his forehead. Quietly. For his shoulders. Quietly. For his legs. Quietly. But all the tears in the world weren't enough for her when it came to his lips. The thin upper one, the thick lower one. To his saliva, which at times smelled like a wine cellar and at others like a tobacco warehouse. Lamentation and wailing. She dressed in black. For his kisses. Avid, tired, weary. For all his kisses. She rubbed ashes into her hair. Even for his kisses not kissed. She fasted. Since a kiss is a word unsaid, the most profound ejaculation, the last breath. Could she live with a man for kisses alone? Yes. With him, yes. Besides, only a kiss can unmask the lies of the flesh, unlock the secrets of the mind, astonish the secrets and the lies of the character. That's why she feels nauseated when she sees a couple kissing at the airport, at sunset, in a car, at parties, outside apartment blocks. Kissing on the cheek, on the forehead, on the hair. Kissing with the concealed eroticism of children and the ideal eroticism of angels. Kissing with the anxious eroticism of couples, who, when one begins a sentence, the other completes it lest tedium should find the time to come out with a few words. Tedium that opens wide the door of fear. Of the fear of habit. Of the fear of silence beside the other. Of the fear of incessant chatter beside the other out of the fear of silence. Yet also of the fear of having second thoughts. Tell me, are you thinking of me at this moment? Of the fear that believes only in miracles. Ah, if only we could wake up as on the first day that I set eyes on you and you on me! Of the fear that believes only in violence. To hell with the man we once gave all our heart to on a plate who threw it into the trash after he'd had his fill of it. She wouldn't stoop to fear these variations on fear that encase more and more fears, likenesses of the most fearful fears, with the fear of the metaphysical trial, with the fear of the necessary evil.

That's why she continued to open her arms and enclose him inside them; him, what should she call him?

Former lover?

Father of the children they never had?

Song of tired devotion?

Curtain.

That same man who now fell into bed like broken branches into a raging flood.

We've gone on long enough. There's no story for us to tell, no story for us to hear. Eventually the heart moves from its place, is catapulted into the darkness of the mind. It dozes between the eyebrows, is restless between the legs. Then the only story you can tell, that you want to hear, is the story that's told by *every man for himself* and that's heard by *everyone out as fast as you can.* Sentences with heart in mouth, words that jostle with each other, as if the one wanted to hide behind the other, silences that deafen you. Which is why the story has no backbone, a cat flattened on the street, leads you nowhere, the wheel of death without death.

Nineteen eighty-eight, second of December, Wednesday, to nineteen ninety-eight, seventh of November, Tuesday. Ten whole years.

The chronicle of a difficult love?

The journal of a weak heart?

The cassette of a branded liar?

A mixture. But, above all, the preparation for a transvestite.

■ ■ ■

You've just seen a man shaving his legs, putting on lipstick, plucking his eyelashes, brushing his hair, padding his breast with cotton wool, sticking down his dick with tape, wearing women's underwear, learning to balance on high heels.

A man masquerading as a woman, to his wife. Not to reverse the roles in bed. Nor to pick up other men. His aim is not to get horny. He masquerades in order to pluck up courage to talk to her. Dirty talk? Not at all. Simply to tell her what he didn't have the courage to say as a man.

Speaking as woman to woman
to his wife.
A transvestite of his wife.
Speaking. For the first
and last time. Speaking
to himself. Face to face.
In his life. A stand-in of him. Speaking.
To Her on his knees.
You, my incurable love
and great heartache.
Eye to eye with Her.
My lovely story
my life's finale.
Appointment under the ground.
Farewell?
Speaking.

Got it off your chest? He couldn't stop the waterworks. Forgive him. He'll return to the world of the expressionless. Don't worry. Can't bear a minute with his crumpled self. Needs people coming and going. Put him in the middle of the marketplace and leave him. Honey-sweet. He should have been a street vendor not a pen pusher. I write, he wrote in his diary, so as not to let myself out of sight. A hundred times. With his hand tied behind him. Letters like hoops. All night long. A night when there's a surfeit of nights, of owl days. I write so as not to let myself out of my sight. A child being punished. Cat, cut, cart. Expelled from the schools of the entire world. Hair shorn. Cat, cut, cart. With ears like cabbages from all the tweaking. With hands like puff pastry from all the whacks. Cat, cut, cart. I write so as not to let myself out of my sight. Tell that tale elsewhere. Cat, cut, cart. You write so as to be out of the sight of someone you don't want to let out of your sight.

He slips away. Disappears into the crowd. He has his way. By covering the paper with flyblows. Pencils down, time's up! Things that can't be said? Acts that can't be seen? Thank heavens for the flyblows. Pencils down, time's up! In any case, isn't reality what remains when we no longer believe in anything beyond what we see? Well, what we see are the flyblows. But do we see what we see or do we see what we are? Pencils down, time's up! Do we see what we see or do we see what we are? That's why he sometimes loses control.

Becomes abrupt. You could even call him a little dictator. Do we see what we see or do we see what we are? The left hand forces the right to write. To write that you can't write is a way to write. He places the pencil between the thumb and forefinger by force. The left paw curses everything holy in order to stop the straight, the regular one from playing this little piggy went to market, from greeting, from waving good-bye, from caressing, from hitting, from slapping, even from gently interlocking with it. To write that you can't write is a way to write. And the right obeys the left. A thrashed dog with its tail between its legs. In any case, there's no face. No possibility of any if you scratch my back, I'll scratch yours and both of us the face, out of the question. Since that face, especially that face, a foxy snout in name and deed, says one thing, thinks another, and does something else. Just once to allow itself to be pinned down and say, Such and such a day, such and such a time. Year and so on. Never. The same curse. Chasing the lost present, the dematerialized here and now. From being a little child. They'd send him on errands and he'd vanish. Whether to the baker's to fetch bread (and dream of the baker's wife kneading him with her breasts) or to the slaughterhouse to buy liver (and to feel his heart palpitate at the squealing and groaning of the animals to be slaughtered) or to the market gardens to choose fresh vegetables (and to peep at the Gypsy girls who lifted their chintz dresses over the braziers). All at the same time. Without a breather. With him left shattered.

And now? A frenzied walk of wagers. Which means? I'm taking for a walk the hole that I'm afraid to look into, that hole that others call *my dearest heart* and others *get thee behind me*. And if I manage to walk across holding my breath and keeping my eyes closed, when

I take a deep breath and open my eyes, I'll be hand in hand with the one precious woman of my life (a little girl with pigtails, two left shoes, and a tart's handbag). And if I don't manage to walk across holding my breath and keeping my eyes closed, I'll have my hand bitten by my old man (a wild beast on his deathbed, a curmudgeon from here to the next world).

And continuing to play at I-spy, knucklebones, tic-tac-toe with himself till he was worn out, till he'd made the streets his home, till he'd discovered a home within his home; a hovel with a light on, a plate of food, a bed to crash in for the jack-in-the-box that had worn the legs off him in all that toing and froing, that joyless toing and froing. Till then, present everywhere and nowhere. Till he pegs out? Time will tell. For the moment, take pleasure in him. Take pleasure in one of his days. Any day at random. All his days. Every day.

Exclusive world premiere. Sincerely, 'kyou.

At daybreak, he's woken by his own snoring. Taking hold of the mini-recorder on the bedside table, he puts it to his lips, like a sick person does a spoonful of medicine.

"I was asleep. I was woken by my snoring. At first I felt frightened, then hard done by. Did I feel like that because there was no one next to me to hug me, just to nudge me so I'd wake up? Or did I feel like that because the moment I woke up, there was a bird with a sheep's fleece, an anteater's snout, and a horse's gaze sitting on my pillow?"

On the morning of the next day, he'll thumb through his old diaries, point with his finger to sentences that he can't remember whether they're his or things said by passersby, or if they're borrowed and unreturned cries of anguish from his reading. Broadly speaking, he divides his days into those that sap him and those that sip him. He shuts his exercise books with his scribbling, in the way that a cat buries its excrement.

He puts in and takes out of his bag five different books, five different notepads, five different printouts of the same manuscript, five different pencils, five different pens. The large or the small camera? The cassette recorder with the sixty-minute or ninety-minute cassette? Whenever he ventures out of his house, he suffers withdrawal symptoms. He misses everything to do with writing, everything to do with reading. It's at such moments that he thinks that in his previous life, instead of footprints, he must have left a snail's slime behind him. A shell study continually on the move.

A little later at the barber's, he'll cock an ear:

"Take a bit less from this side . . ."

"Instead of trying to improve your looks, you'd do far better to find yourself a wife for your old age."

"I've got a wife . . ."

"What wife, when we all know she died last year?"

On the trolley, a man with a freckled face leans over to him and whispers in his ear: "A respectable man never talks about himself." He's annoyed by those random words from the random passenger. He changes his seat in a huff as if that casual saying had been directed at him.

Just as he's getting off at the Panepistimiou Street stop, he reads on the wall of the Catholic church the words I MADE A MISTAKE, BUT IN THE END I WAS PROVED RIGHT. He wonders whether, if boredom is the one pole of his temperament, is the other shyness? He feels shyness and boredom. Boredom and shyness. Is he bored because he's shy? Is he shy because he's bored? Is he afraid to be shy and that's why he's bored? Is he afraid of being bored and that's why he's shy? Is he afraid and that's why, at the same time, he's both afraid and shy?

He pushes open the door of Zonar's without unraveling the tangled thread of his thought. Sitting opposite him, next to the café window, is a portly middle-aged man with blue eyes and a neat, sandy-colored beard. Wearing gloves, he's underlining line by line the texts of a foreign-language newspaper in front of him. Just as he decides that this fellow could embody the central character in one of his stories, the man leaves his tea half-finished as if someone had tried to poison him. A relay race, he tightens the thread of his previous thought: when will the pole of boredom and when will the pole of shyness break, and I'll be found buried under the ruins of this defective passion?

Walking down Evripidou Street, intoxicated by the aromas of all the mountain herbs, gazing at the sacks and the colorful glass vases, he'll follow on the heels of some wayside wretch.

The autobiographer of the present tense stares profoundly at the asphalt, as if stumbling at every step over something valuable. Every so often, he mutters to himself, "I sigh at everything lost to me. Where should I begin and where end? I'm called Michael and my name is Faïsides. A stake is plunged in my heart. While we go on talking, we're losing our hair, losing our teeth, losing time. Losing in general."

At the corner of Metaxa and Benaki Streets, coming out of the office of the literary magazine where he'd just left his monthly article, two junkies give their own performance.

The girl, pierced with safety pins from head to toe, on bended knee, begs the man for the dose she needs urgently. He, with two dull pearls in place of his eyes and stumbling about, tries to keep it from her. The girl follows him on her knees, wailing out loud. He drives her away, hitting out at the air. They look as if they're moving in jam.

His daily walk will come to an end at Dyros. He'll order lentil soup, olives, feta, brown bread and half a liter of white wine. At the opposite table, a well-dressed woman with thick gray hair has just finished eating. She wipes her mouth with the napkin, takes a drink of water, and lights a cigarette. Her movements are peculiarly slow, as if the slowness alleviates something gnawing away at her insides. Suddenly, as if she'd forgotten her good manners, she sticks her finger into her mouth. At first she carefully feels her teeth as if they're hurting her. Then she madly rubs her gums. Next she sticks out her tongue, and, like a child that's smeared itself with chocolate, she licks the area around her mouth. Her eyelids grow heavy. Eventually, she removes one of her shoes and lets her hands fall limp at her side.

He feels the need to get up from his seat, shake her, slap her even, just so long as he rouses her out of her confined public sensuousness.

In the end he just shuts his eyes. A tattered dream takes hold of him. He's staring at a crooked bed. A man is sleeping there, curled up. He turns in his sleep. Mingling together with his breathing are sounds that oscillate between sobs and creaking boards. The man turns over on his other side. The pillow's hybrid bird paces up and down in the room. A black bird with a hunched back and the stride of a giant is shaken by the sobbing. His tears have wet the sheets, caused the walls to swell, caused the ceiling to collapse. Kilograms of tears. Indescribable wailing.

Before getting back home to Vyronas, before getting the key into the door, he'll see without seeing, hear without hearing, think without thinking:

1. "The moth is born on the 16th of May," reveals a man without legs, with well-groomed sideburns, to a dog keeping him company while he begs outside the Russian Church.

2. On a bench in Zappeion Park, a gray and shriveled woman says to another woman who's staring at her shoes with eyes popping out of her head: "He made a doormat of my heart, the old consumptive, a doormat!"

3. Glass panes shattering, pigeons cooing, cackling in droves, horns, someone coughing like a wolf, screeching brakes, a deep sigh.

4. All the children of mutilated families hate holidays and festive days, free days. For the offspring of this failed legion, the coin in the cake, the painted eggs, the flag flying, the carnival masks are anniversaries of silences, quarrels, settlements.

5. He realizes that he clears his nose just like his father (covering it with his entire hand and picking it with his finger); that he smokes just like his mother (holding the smoke for a few seconds in his mouth before exhaling it with relief, as if he'd found the solution to some vexing problem); that he never goes to bed if there's a half-open cupboard in the house (just like his father); that he finds money in clothes he hasn't worn for a long time (just like his mother), etc.

6. "Happiness is dying at the same moment as your daddy, at the same moment as your mommy." That's what one little girl says to another little girl. The two children are playing blissfully on the swings.

7. Three swarthy types are talking as if they were swallowing loukoumades. When anyone goes near them, they converge around the notional circle delineated by their bodies. In this way, they protect their hunger, their loneliness, their language, their destiny.

8. "Money never sleeps," mutters a man who's turned out the pockets of his ragged trousers and ragged jacket in a polite but desperate attempt to prove to the passersby, to himself, to the phantoms that he has nothing to hide—neither inside him nor on him.

9. Three men at the stop in front of the Olympic Stadium mop the tiredness and sorrow from their faces with their shirt sleeves, all at the same time. The first one's lips are cracked like a roast chestnut. The second one's eyes are so dilated that they give the impression that if he doesn't hold his head up straight, the eyeball will pop out of the outline of his face. The third man's cheeks flap like fans cooling the place.

Inserting the key in the door, he recognizes his father's voice on the answering machine. The short, disheartening, almost aggressive messages left by his father could be the first lines of short, disheartening, almost aggressive monologues. "Nothing new, all old stuff. Do you hear? Very old stuff." "Cold, cold enough for your parents." "I'm ready for the grave. Give me a call." "Out again? I'm tired of talking to this machine."

While putting on his pajamas, he reflects that of late, his life from the waist down is regulated by an idealistic perversion. He inveterately chases after girls much younger than he. He adds beads to the rosary of an ascetic licentiousness. A cantankerous old rake with the snout of an incurable skirt chaser. Which is why if any of the nymphets give in to him, he beats a retreat, annoyed, offended, often overcome by panic. As if the same girls who earlier enticed him with their youth and innocence suddenly become old from the very moment that they surrender to him; turn into hags whose only aim is to surround him with little brats, to drown him in worries.

Which explains his post-event fear. That's why before the women passing through his bed can light up a cigarette, wash, come out with the usual small talk and leave him in peace, he shuts his eyes tight, presses his temples, and rubs his neck. His declared cervical syndrome doesn't only have its downside. Deep down he wishes that his transitory companion would shoot off like a rocket in some unknown direction.

The only girl to escape from the pendulum of lust-tedium is Grigoria Samsiadou. Ria is his neighbor and a failed actress. On her dead father's pension, mother, daughter and mynah bird just manage to make ends meet in a three-room apartment exactly below his. In the living room, the mother, bloated from all the medicines, opens and closes the sofa bed each day. Ria has turned her child's room into an acting studio. The couple's former bedroom has been turned into a tiny mausoleum. The suits, shoes, newspaper, and briefcase of the departed lawyer remain untouched, exactly where he left them when he used to get dressed, tie his laces, read his newspaper, and pick up his briefcase. Only the mynah bird circulates unconcerned in the rooms of both living and dead, monotonously repeating, "I'm not a bird."

He once browsed through her lined exercise book, where in large childlike letters with long tails, she wrote:

What have you done with it? I don't know, I've lost it. Again? Again. I don't remember. Leave me alone. Pale colors. Mainly pink. And some yellows, a warm yellow. Cotton, woolen cardigans. A whole year. She was in the fourth year of elementary school.

One cardigan each week. Though she knew that the cardigans weren't lost, she acted as if they were. That's why her heart was on the point of breaking at her mother's harsh remonstrations, that's why she found refuge in her daddy's loving embrace. She wasn't aware of this, though she sensed it. A dangerous lie is a convincing lie. The lie that, because of its depth, leads the one who's lying to get angry if you tell him to his face you're a common liar. As at the same time he thinks you're doing him a blatant injustice, believing that he's the only one with access to the plain truth, that he's the only one who embodies it.

She herself was certain about the disappearance of the cardigans that she herself threw, every morning for a whole year, into the boiler room of the apartment block. Which is why, when the caretaker discovered them, twelve cardigans all the same color, moldy green, and called on her parents to inform them of his incredible find, she was taken aback. Not so much because all the suspicion fell on her, with the result that her mother slapped her and her father gazed at her in bewilderment. What had terrified her was that this inexplicable act weighed heavily upon a person very close to her; a person about whom she cared excessively; a person who influenced her every action and her every thought, and yet a person about whom she'd lost all hope, a person who was incorrigible, who couldn't be either coaxed or coerced.

Which is why, from the time she was a little girl, she'd always liked the color of the ascomycetous fungus of the genus *penicillium*, the terre verte of the painters, the chromatic scale of putrescence in wood, in water, in edibles.

And this was the main reason she left her sandwiches in her schoolbag to decompose. Besides, mold gave things a joyful appearance, not at all repulsive. In any case, the stench of the stifled damp didn't turn her stomach. Till eventually her exercise books and pens started to smell, her pencil case was permeated, and, terrified, her classmates and her teacher began searching the classroom and wondering what on earth could be smelling like a dead dog. Then her cheeks glowed. Her blue eyes took on the most innocent expression. Her lips quietly hummed a song with incomprehensible words.

The song of mold. It was to this that she attuned her whole life, that [. . .]

Anyhow, that afternoon, he was in no mood to see Ria. An unbearable headache had been tormenting him since the morning. Endless hot water bottles on the back of his neck, endless massage with analgesic ointments, endless soluble powders. The pain was splitting his head in two. Nevertheless, he kept thinking about funny scenes with himself in the leading role. He wanted to roll on the floor with laughter but was unable. As if the right side of his head took pleasure in seeing the left side suffering.

Just one typical example.

He must have been about fifteen. They were moving house and

his mother, her lover, and his father were all helping. On pulling out the washing machine, the ancient triangle of family union found itself before a rich archive of pornographic stories in which author, protagonist, and reader were identified. In the private aphrodisiac scripts, spotted with dried stains, relatives and friends were tangled together in unbelievable combinations.

With one thing and another, at the last minute he just managed to catch *Together Again*—his own television news bulletin.

This time two women and a man are ripping into each other. Supposedly they are laying claim to the memory and love of someone deceased. All this for the screen. Behind the screen, they are parading their family ills and selling them for a pretty price.

FATHER-IN-LAW: When did you stop wearing black?
DAUGHTER-IN-LAW: What does it look like I'm wearing now?
FATHER-IN-LAW: Where, here? And when you're at home, out and about in cafés?
DAUGHTER-IN-LAW: When are you ever in my home to see what I wear?
MOTHER-IN-LAW: The whole of Paiania is talking about it. It's not even a year since Liakos went, and you're no longer in black. So much for your love. It's shameful. You're shameful.
DAUGHTER-IN-LAW: You're the one who should be ashamed. And you dare to call me shameful. As for your love for Liakos, don't make me open my mouth.
MOTHER-IN-LAW: Open your mouth?
DAUGHTER-IN-LAW: Yes, open my mouth. Don't make me.
FATHER-IN-LAW: Do you think we're afraid of your dirty mouth?

MOTHER-IN-LAW: Leave her, she'll have another one of her fits.

DAUGHTER-IN-LAW: Fits . . . me?

MOTHER-IN-LAW: You froth at the mouth, don't you?

DAUGHTER-IN-LAW: Me? Froth at the mouth?

MOTHER-IN-LAW: You roll around on the floor, don't you?

DAUGHTER-IN-LAW: Me? Roll around on the floor?

MOTHER-IN-LAW: From the time you were single. Before Liakos. He used to bring you pills by the handful.

DAUGHTER-IN-LAW: I'm not going to start talking . . .

MOTHER-IN-LAW: What do you mean you're not going to talk. That's what we've come here for, to talk.

FATHER-IN-LAW: Talk, what are you waiting for? We've got nothing to be afraid of.

DAUGHTER-IN-LAW: Was Liakos pill popping or wasn't he?

MOTHER-IN-LAW: Just be careful what you say, the whole of Greece is watching us.

DAUGHTER-IN-LAW: You were the ones who wanted me to talk . . .

FATHER-IN-LAW: And there's a God who's listening to your foul mouth . . . Show a bit of respect for my gray hair. Show some respect for our grief.

DAUGHTER-IN-LAW: You weren't thinking of your gray hair when you started touching me up.

MOTHER-IN-LAW: What's that you said?

DAUGHTER-IN-LAW: Don't pretend you don't know.

MOTHER-IN-LAW: Did my husband try it on with you?

DAUGHTER-IN-LAW: He didn't try it on, he got it on.

MOTHER-IN-LAW: My husband?

DAUGHTER-IN-LAW: Yours!

FATHER-IN-LAW: Let her get it out. That spite. Let her. Otherwise, she'll spite herself.

MOTHER-IN-LAW: No, I'm not going to let it go like that. Did my husband try it on with you? I'm asking you.

DAUGHTER-IN-LAW: Why do you think he and Liakos came to blows last year?

MOTHER-IN-LAW: So you're bringing our son into it now, are you?

DAUGHTER-IN-LAW: Are you going to answer my question?

MOTHER-IN-LAW: Anyway, what can you expect? Liakos took you in off the street.

DAUGHTER-IN-LAW: Are you going to answer or shall I?

MOTHER-IN-LAW: He met you in a bar.

DAUGHTER-IN-LAW: He got it on with me. He got it on with me, and you know it.

MOTHER-IN-LAW: I love her, Mom. Come and meet her folks. But you only met her yesterday, Son, and today you're going to ask for her hand?

DAUGHTER-IN-LAW: You turned a blind eye. So you wouldn't lose him.

MOTHER-IN-LAW: Mom, she's a good girl, you'll see. Good, you say, she's covered in tattoos . . .

DAUGHTER-IN-LAW: Just like you knew about your best friend and your sister.

MOTHER-IN-LAW: I'll have her get rid of them, Mom, you'll see.

DAUGHTER-IN-LAW: He cheated on you. Slapped you about, too. The whole lot of you sharing the same bed.

MOTHER-IN-LAW: We'll all live together, Mom, you'll see. I'll have her get rid of them.

He turns off the television. The presenter doesn't appear. He talks from a huge screen. He interrupts, advises, admonishes, consoles. But above all, he stokes the hatred, stirs up the past, opens old wounds. God of his guests' humiliation and demi-god of the viewing figures companies, he has the right résumé. A former Maoist and neo-orthodox, a passionate anti-American and anti-European from the ranks of the independent radio, hand in glove with the Socialist Party in the heyday of private radio. Often on center stage, in between the butchering of his guests, he comes out with populist oratory of the kind that is music to many leftist-rightist ears.

He turns on the radio. Low. Just loud enough to hear. Music or talk? Ceaseless static in his ears. From the time when the stammer sealed his mouth, securing a bright future for him as a dumb observer, he'd sought deafness's humming. His current fear? That he might start to gibber. That he might start to argue with himself in public, become a laughingstock, and that hush-hush turn into unbridled chatter.

Gazing at his face in the bathroom mirror, he swallows a Seroxat and two Lexotanil without water. He puts the Walkman's headphones over his ears. In the elevator, he slaps himself, first playfully, then hard. He presses the play button to start the cassette with Bach's *Saint Matthew Passion*, the Sephardic songs, and the popular hits by Takis Soukas. He walks along the street as if his clothes had caught fire. His every step a Witsetzenunsin Tranenniederay dutmitemialmadurmitemivistayoucallmelovebutIamnotyour love

his step
every

    one.

When his legs can no longer support him, he hails the first taxi to pass. Before he even has time to say good evening, I want to go to such-and-such a place to the taxi driver, the driver says, "He killed her. Sprinkled a sick lamb with parathion and left it beside the river. And you can't say I hadn't warned her. Keep away from dead animals that dogs or wolves don't go near. You see, she was overjoyed because of our firstborn. And she forgot. As soon as she'd eaten it, she spewed up a yellow liquid. The sun was coming down thick like blood when she folded her wings. When she'd gone to sleep for good, I chopped her into pieces and scattered her high up in the rocks. Let her brothers find her, let them eat her. For five whole days I never budged from the roost. On the sixth day, I couldn't endure it any longer. I came down to eat something. When I went back, I found only the shells. I thought of getting myself shot by hunters. But as soon as I saw the ferret running alongside the river, I fell on it and smashed its skull. That same afternoon I flew over the murderer's sheepfold. In the air I wrote, *you're going to die.* He thought I was making a reconnaissance flight to find food. He penned in his flock and kept a hold of his shotgun. At first light, I fell on him like a rocket. He'd gone to take a shit and I found him unprotected. At the moment I was swallowing his eye, her little soul rejoiced inside me. Since then, I've fallen apart. I eat with a heavy heart, I fly with a heavy heart, I sleep with a heavy heart. Because I'm called *Aegypius monachus*, so the encyclopedias say."

This narration by the man with the face of a boxer and the voice of a cantor was interrupted by a big powerful motorbike that cut in front of him. "Where are you going?" he asks me, after cursing the biker to high heaven. "I don't know," I answer. "I'll take you wherever you want, even to where you don't know. No charge. So long as you let me tell you two more stories. You know, I've lost all faith in people. I feel safer with animals. Besides, we're returning to the animal. That's why my heroes are exclusively animals."

While passing in front of the Parliament building, the taxi driver, who isn't a taxi driver but a failed writer of children's books, told him the story of a brown bear from the brutal years of the Civil War. Before ending up as a skin in front of the armchair of the English commissioner, the omnivorous beast had smelled "Miseria," the partisan, shot by his own hand and dismembered by a hand grenade in the mountains of Roumeli. Then, leaving behind them the underworld realm of Kerameikos cemetery, he began to tell him the story of the fox who admired the Roman mosaics in Dion. Before the archaeologists' spades had uncovered the place. Entering through a burrow that it dug itself. The art-loving chicken thief was hanged by three Albanian workers. Evil-faced, hungry, and frightened. They hanged it on an arbutus tree. Not knowing any other way of being more callous than the director of the excavations, who, when payday came, turned them over to the authorities as illegal immigrants.

It was as clear as day that the weird taxi driver had his books printed at his own expense. For what parent would buy his child tales in which the main characters were all embittered vultures, skinned bears, and hanged foxes?

And so, story after story, animal after animal, requiem after requiem, he drove him all around the capital without turning on the meter. Eleusis, the ancient Kerameikos cemetery, Psyrri, Omonoia Square, the quarries at Vyronas. Finally, he parked outside his house. He lifted him up like featherdown and, hugging him as his parents had never hugged him, he put him to bed.

Then. A little before, a little after. It's no longer of any importance. He'll open his eyes. There's no question of that. He won't see his nose and yet he'll see. As sure as I can see you. He'll see. He'll prop himself on his elbows and sit up. Will he arrange the pillow behind his head? Will he throw a cardigan over his shoulders? Will he poke around for his slippers with his feet? Details, details. So very many have lost their lives delving into details. At times motionless, as if they'd been hypnotized on their feet, at other times darting about, as if they had a pack of wolves at their heels. Because, of course, this is what you have to go through if you begin to add up everything you know and don't know about him. Seven lives aren't enough. You can talk yourself hoarse and there's still no end to it. Not to mention that often what you never learn about him is, nevertheless, something you know deep down the way you know the back of your hand; this raises its head, stamps its feet, froths at the mouth, breaks things, with the result that by compulsion you become his seer. Wonderful prospect. Get it into your thick head. Eventually you're going to have to learn to follow him at a distance. All the familiarity, the gushing is over. Forget everything you know. He's not even your closest chum for you to open up to, or a game for you to pass your time. He's the straw you drew. Short? Short. Fat? Fat. Hairy? Hairy. Accept him. You're veritable lovebirds, and you want to change him? Sometimes you're filled with spite. You go to the other extreme. You exclude him from your thoughts, you expel him from your heart. You eat together like strangers, sleep together as after a quarrel. Good morning, good night. At night you hear him pacing up and down. He smokes, sighs, turns the radio on full, farts shamelessly, shouts the names of the dead, plays with his willy, weeps. What kind of life is that? Accept it, he's not for you. You know how it is when you're sitting with your father at the hospital? Sunday afternoons. The television on. The sun refusing to go down. Your father going on about people's lost humanity. The artificial kidney machine gurgling. Something like that. Search for the analogies. The pattern.

So let's sum up. Every detail has its right time. Then. He opens his eyes. Night. In the middle, at the end, at the beginning. Anyway darkness. He opens his eyes. And sees. Ultraviolet rays? A dream within a dream? Reincarnation of a feline? Lots happening. If you're in the mood. Anyway, before he decides to open his eyes, or rather before he opens them, as we don't know if there's any decision, he feels the way he does when he gets up at daybreak for a pee. When, stumbling about, he flops back into bed. When he gropes at the doors, the furniture, the walls. When he walks like someone blind, certain that if he opens his eyes wide, if the sleep leaves his eyes, some form of doom will befall him. A terrible earthquake with him as the sole survivor. A phone call from the other world. His own self coming into the room and asking him for forgiveness, after first beating him mercilessly. Things like that. Eschatology, that's laughable. Anyhow. Let's not confuse things. Then. He opens his eyes, and so on. He begins walking. On the ceiling. Back and forth. Miles and miles. Covering incredible distances. Coming and going. A box four by seven holds everything. Provided your legs can take it.

When he gets tired, he leans up against the walls. He puts his hands behind his head and stretches, as if he were sprawled out on the grass. Then once more from the beginning. Aimless walking till his pins can no longer hold him. Then stretched out again. Without his having lost his sense of gravity. Without his having taken hallucinogenic drugs. Without, and the most nauseous of all, his thinking in poetic images. Everyday things, almost commonplace. Things that could happen to anyone. Provided you accept being bound hand and foot by your own self. Because, of course, if you're a captive of your own self, the only thing that remains to you is not to trust anyone. Not even your self, when it feigns indifference, cynicism, even death. Naturally, a quick solution so you'll grow sick of the one feigning indifference, cynicism, and death is to keep talking to him. To shut your ears to any sound other than that whispered prattling with your self. To succeed in this, you cut the telephone cord, swallow the key to the apartment, throw the television and radio from the balcony, hoard nuts, and begin to write. Or better, you listen for the voice that comes from the *no farther*. For years now. From the world above and below. Identical. Tongue-wagging from the cradle. A grouch right to the grave. Your life's text in every detail. An imposter's written destiny. Lousy, whore-spawned, cankerous. Words. Words that no power can knock any sense into. Neither a kind phrase, nor the habit of no longer meaning anything, nor what's to follow: *not a word.* But eventually you get tired of climbing on the ceiling, of rolling on the floor, of scraping against the walls. You get tired of seeing the room rotating like the big wheel at a fun fair and you decide to get down to it and write. Then you set aside the lousy, whore-spawned, cankerous words. You dip the pen, your finger, your nose, your dick into your excretions. With the excrement the more dramatic parts, with the tears the more hilarious ones. And you rewrite what you've lived, what you haven't lived, what you lived once and for all, what you'll live and go on living for life, what you don't realize you're living while you're living it, what lives between what you've lived and what you haven't lived, what everybody lives, what nobody lives, what lives opposed to life, what in life is not life, what lives beyond life, what lives prior to life.

What was that you said? A song that's incontinent? Whatever you say. A sickly novel? Speak up, go on. Stories that consume their own flesh? Agreed. Whatever the fox can't do, it turns into a tale. And that's only the half of it. Just shut your mouth, that's all. What? Put a sock in it. What was that you said? Shut it. Shut it, or else I'll bury you alive. I'll do you in. I'll make mincemeat of you. I'll slice you up. Understand? First I'll tear you apart, then I'll eat you up and spit you out. Do I make myself clear? How else do you want me to say it? Not a word. You'll listen, that's all. Because you've made it your aim to see me roaming the streets all day selling paper handkerchiefs. MOTHER DEAD FROM HEART. FATHER EPILEPTIC. FIVE BROTHERS AND SISTERS. NO BREAD TO EAT. ONLY ONE ARM. And in the evening, making a bundle of whatever coins I've collected for dirty phone calls. C'MON YOU HORNY BABE. THAT'S MY BIG BOY. MY PUSSY'S ALL WET. FUCK ME SENSELESS. GIVE IT TO ME. GIVE IT TO ME LIKE THERE'S NO TOMORROW.

So. Enough of crosswords that lead to more crosswords. Across the comedy of pain. Down the tyranny of originality. In between in all the black squares, love expires companionless. No solution is going to get your socks washed, massage you, light a candle for you.

The moment's come. We've put it. The period. The very last one. After that, *ashes to ashes, dust to dust.*

So, I've had my fill of self. That crossroads of violence gets you nowhere. I'll return to the Jewish quarter. Had . . . my . . . fill . . .

My grandfather was known as *laughter of the soul*, my father as *father of many nations*, I myself as *what God is like to you!* Clutching the circumcised hypophysis, I'll find myself in the cobbled streets. Clutching my dick, as I'll never clutch the little hand of a child or grandchild, as my own mother's or father's paw never clutched mine, I'll lead myself into the yard of the demolished synagogue. *Bar'chu et Adonai ham'vorach.* To hell with the trembling in the mouth. *Baruch Adonai ham'vorach l'olam va'ed.* I'll read from the *Perasa*. In any case, rabbi, thirteen-year-old, and relatives, the same person. Gray-haired with cervical syndrome and insomnia. *Baruch atah Adonai, eloheinu melech ha'olam, asher bachar banu mikol ha'amim, v'natan lanu et torato, Baruch atah Adonai notein hatorah.* Definitely no time for kippah and talith. *Baruch atah Adonai, eloheinu melech ha'olam, asher natan lanu torat emet, v'chayei olam nata b'tocheinu, Baruch atah Adonai notein hatorah.* Son of the Law with thirty years' delay. Better late than never. Witnesses? Cats, lizards, thistles, and used condoms. In any case, everything else was reconciled with the idea of Zyklon B.

Afterward, I'll keep a minute's silence. The candle stuck in the face. I might not be able to breathe. A handful of ashes for a heart. I might close my eyes. Testicles of soap. Keep me away from metaphysical effronteries. Just the capital up front of a life coming to an end. Which explains the candle stuck in the face, a handful of ashes for a heart, the testicles of soap.

I'll halt here. A fool for solitude. Before the unthinkable toll begins in the city of coal, before the trains are packed for Dobnitsa and then Lom, before the sinking of the Karageorgi riverboat and the stirring of the black mud in the mid-European Danube. I'll halt here. Solomon Kasevi, insurance broker, Moïs Romano, timber merchant, Raphael Karaso, owner of a sesame-oil mill, Solomon Youda, leather merchant, Mordis Kasavi, ironsmith, Mair Dasas, tobacco merchant, Isaac Bensour, hatter, Isaac David, hotelier, Joseph Levi, pharmacist (president of the Israelite Community), Isaac Hasdak, tailor. Then when the voices of the muezzin, of the priest and the rabbi passed like a cross-stitch on endless fabric, with the crescent moon, the sign of the cross, and the star of David gushing cool water. Before the names sank into oblivion's downy mold. Samuel Hatzi, dried-fruits merchant, Israel Kazes, moneychanger, Nisem Osmos, glass merchant, René Bensoua, transport company owner, Alboher Behar, maid, Thaleia Sarda, midwife, Roza Negrin, Ventura Perla, housekeeping, Yedo Eskenazy, infant, Abraham Alboher, infant, Joseph Benouzio, infant, Clara Baroka, infant—

All those names. Biblical stories, place names from Iberia, corruptions of German words, Muslim trades. All those names. Written on the back of postcards of big European cities.

It will be night then. A gentle night. Landscapes of silken darkness will open, unfold, surround the synagogue. Meanwhile, the menorah will flicker in all the windows. Hooked noses and ebony-black locks will outline the basic scenes of the race on the wall. The centuries' shadow theater. How was it that Moses carved the Commandments on slabs of stone because he had a stutter? How was it that in 5352, the sixteenth of the month of Av and a Friday, the distant ancestors all packed into sixteen large caravels? How was it that one night before daybreak in Ashkenaz the world turned upside down and the dead found themselves walking like the living, while the living found themselves under the ground flailing their arms and legs, as if someone had pinned them to the floor?

That night, the *noche judia*, my Yids will fart en masse. Their

farts will smell of stewed cabbage, matzoth and tagiko, their farts
will become a lute, dulcimer, tambourine, guitar, horn and they'll
play an old song of Seville; a melancholic ballad hidden deep in the
heart like the uprooted mezuzah in the pocket . . .

> To leave for that plain is all I want
> I'll leave for that plain.
> For bread I'll have the wild grass
> for water my tears.
> With my nails I'll dig
> with my blood I'll water
> with my breath I'll dry.
> In the heart of that plain
> I'll build a hut:
> on the outside reed and lime
> inside I'll daub it with soot.
> Whoever loses his way
> will find a shelter there
> and he'll tell me his troubles
> and I'll tell him my troubles.
> And if mine are more
> I'll persevere in life
> and if his are more
> with my own hands I'll kill myself
> with my very own hands
> oh, I'll kill myself!

Lady Cortisol

In memory of Nikos Panayotopoulos

Eventually, he'll ask you, *Do you live alone or with your parents? With my parents?* you'll ask yourself along with him. The repetition of the question always gives rise to something in the one asking, something between excitement, puzzlement, irritation — and at precisely the moment that he feels you to be his echo, you, stalling for time, more carefully prepare what it is you want to say, though, to be exact, very exact, these assumptions concern the rule, whereas the one asking you is the embodiment of the exception of exceptions. At any rate, if you decide to tell him straight out, *You know, my parents have been deceased for quite a few years*, you automatically exclude the possibility at some other time, when you feel more frank, more forthcoming, perhaps even more dynamic, in other words when you have your feet more firmly on the ground, of coming out with *Yes, I've been living with my bedridden mother these past five years*, and, subsequently, lowering the tone of your voice, of murmuring, *Tell me, is that so bad?* or *Am I doing anything bad?* However, most probably you'll abandon that line too and say to him, *In one sense at least, don't we all live with our parents always?* And because you don't expect any answer from him, first because your question is a rhetorical one, and second because he, especially he, is the last one to give an answer to anything, given that he was born, exists for as long as he exists, and will expire with a question on his lips, taking up your line of thought again you'll continue by saying, *Even when they're dead. Especially then. Perhaps we're even closer then. Because when they're alive we might be separated by a dividing wall, we might live near them or miles away, we might be on bad terms or good, but when they die, the reasons for being close or distant disappear. And it's then that the real living together begins. It's then that you hear your dad, hear him as though the two of you were together, in the same room, like then, as he shuffles his slippers or as the newspaper falls from his hands when he falls asleep in the armchair. It's then that you see your mom staring at her face in the mirror; maybe you stand slightly behind her, without touching her, without looking at your reflection, as with slow, very slow movements, she spreads the moisturizing cream on her cheeks, on her brow, on the wrinkles below her neck, as though with that delaying tactic she were trying to hypnotize, to anesthetize time, so that it will overlook her, forget her, stop drying her skin and wrinkling her body, in other words, stop ruining her existence.* And if because of this answer, he thinks you're weird, morbid, conceited, or who knows what else, you can say something to him that perhaps will surprise him, even if he's not usually surprised: *Listen, I left home at sixteen, shook the dust off my feet. I moved between cities, jobs, and men till I became what I became. When I saw them again it was in their coffins. All decked out. My dad with white carnations, my mom with white roses. My dad with the same supercilious smile, in his brown suit, my mom with that same expression of sad perplexity in her sky-blue dress with the cream collar and the same border around the cuffs. I could even say, without deviating an iota from the anatomical exactitude, that they didn't miss me at all, that it was as if I hadn't been gone for even a minute from the house in which I was born, in which I'd first seen the light of day. And since we're on the subject, was it I wonder on a dry pale afternoon in a stone house by the sea, amid banana trees and palms? Or was it on a chill milky morning high up in the mountains, in a wooden two-story house, buried among maples and oaks? But most probably I was born in a dirty, noisy hovel in the middle of nowhere, in which a sliver of light bathed everything from dawn to dusk.* Something like that. Of course all this will happen given that he asks you this and not something more general, more vague, in order to trap you, forcing you to be more precise, more tangible, more concrete. For example, if he asks, *Do you watch the news, are you interested in current affairs? Are you or aren't you a woman of your times?* Here you have to watch out. It requires careful handling. Maybe you'll even have to remain silent. Not too long so as not to appear rude, anxious, or scheming. Just as long as it takes. Just as long as it takes for him to perceive the voluntary sealing of your lips as a sign of responsibility and verbal precision. Then, and after your breast has gently heaved a few times in the meantime, you'll say to him, *Any news that I manage to avoid is a gain. I'm speaking with hand on heart. I can't bear that daily update. Soldiers are always going to kill and be killed, politicians are always going to lie and be indifferent to ordinary people, bankers are only going to smile when their pockets are full, artists will constantly confuse the reality they have in their heads with the reality that exists outside their heads. I go to sleep with the expectation, when I awake, of finding things more stable, more settled, I don't mean outside time, and more eternal.* But because, not such a rare phenomenon, we say something and at the same time feel the very opposite of what we just stated and maintained, whether half-heartedly or passionately—these things are also a matter of judgment—you'll say to him, *Generally speaking, I feel completely ephemeral and transient, stuck in an uneventful here and now. Indeed I'm at a loss, more than a loss, I'm actually annoyed, bowled over, by those who make plans for the future or return to things of the past. Expectations and reminiscences are absent from my horizon. I indulge myself with the present, a present passionately in love with itself. Yes, I dream of my present.* This is what you'll say, although deep inside something is gnawing at you: a footnote, an asterisk, a memo of a memo. Besides, wasn't it these infinitesimal things, these capillaries, that kept ruining your life all your life? The things that don't appear. And the less they appear, the more they determine, poison, erode the things that do appear, that stand out, that overly appear. At any rate, if you want to be clear, to be accurate with only minimal divergence from what is actually the case, you'll admit, reveal to him, that quite often you read old newspapers. In other words, you'll say to him, *I'm fascinated, totally absorbed by stale news. All that mustiness about it, all that information after the event, relaxes me. And I'm not referring to major events, to events that change the world—usually for the worse—but to the minor ones, the unimportant, inconsequential ones. Catastrophes or little farces, grave or ridiculous events, on a small scale. Those that, in a weird sort of way, reveal just how slowly, almost uneventfully, life, our simple daily life, changes. And take note, and I want to stress this, I'm not saying I reread, I'm saying I read, because I'm getting the news for the first time, after the event, naturally. And that's strange. Unusual. I feel as though I'm browsing backward through the days, as if surprised by a fait accompli, as if turning the hands of the clock counterclockwise, while at the same time I reflect that time has passed, as though it hadn't passed at all, as though Zeno's notorious arrow were poking fun at me.* And before you're able to recover from the wave of the previous question, before your reply can settle, before you can finally satisfy your relentless questioner, the bewildered woman respondent, or the indifferent question, he unleashes the next one, *Tell me, do you get tired easily or not?* Without giving it much thought, you'll answer, *What can I say now— I'm, dare I say, tireless, yes, I'm indefatigable. Most likely I have the gene of tirelessness. How else can I put it—I have to tire myself excessively or be subjected to something extreme for me to feel, as they say, done in or ready to drop. Otherwise, there's no other reason.* And just as you're about to fall silent, to remain a few seconds with yourself, alone, to take a breath, you pass over to the other bank and in a calm voice, perhaps enriched with veins of apathy, you say to him, *Of course there are days, whole weeks, even months, long periods, rarely, it's true, when everything tires me. Just the very act of breathing makes me feel as if I've dug a huge pit. Of course, here we're getting into a big topic—pit I could say. Labyrinthine. But I don't want to go on about it too much. There's tiredness and tiredness, tiredness of tiredness, as well as tiredness without tiredness—that's real tiredness. Someone moves a heavy cupboard, breaks his back doing it, and, wiping his brow with the back of his hand, mutters to himself, "I'm tired." And he means it. But "I'm tired" is also said by the woman who returns home after a late night out, after a reunion of old classmates. Her stomach is taut, her temples are about to burst. Not from the food or alcohol, but because she met up with all those former boys and girls, all those former loud and bubbly young kids, who are now standing before her overweight, shy, arrogant, depressed, or disheartened—in other words, battered and bruised, as though maltreated by time's rough hand. And yet she, striving to find rhyme or reason in the sudden loss of her young husband as a result of an aneurysm, still being so young herself, so unbearably young, declares she's tired, chronically exhausted. Which is why the only thing she can find to comfort her, to really give her some rest, is the leap she takes from the balcony of her apartment building, preceded by several leaps from her inner, unseen balcony, but this last leap, the irreversible one, is what gives rhyme or reason, what alleviates once and for all loss's irremovable, fearful void. Nevertheless, there's also an unjustifiable exhaustion, hanging over, without seeds, as if it were coming out of nowhere and going nowhere. In other words, no connection at all with the exhaustion that is found in a lack of mercury, magnesium, iron, and selenium. This clandestine, intangible exhaustion is found in an excessive amount of organized life, architectured peace, systematic avoidance of cracks and discontinuity. With the result that, while you're sitting in your garden sipping your espresso or your margarita, gazing at your husband pruning the rosebushes and your children playing and frolicking, zing, zing, zing. Or while you're getting out of your car, shining and satisfied because of a difficult contract you've secured for the company you work for, a contract that with mathematical precision will send your salary rocketing as well as giving you a step up in your professional field, zing, zing, zing. Even on your birthday, when you're at a Mexican restaurant with the gals, with all your close buddies, and you're getting ready to blow out the candles on the huge Mexican cake, zing, zing, zing. When everything is going smoothly, everything appears free of care, everything augurs for the best. Zing, zing, zing. And down she goes. As if something jolts you. As if you've taken hold of a live wire with wet hands. Zing, zing, zing. And with the trembling of a slight electric shock and with slightly singed fingers*

and eyebrows, you realize, no more just in words and theory, that behind the conciliatory, organized, peace-loving tiredness, boiling,
bubbling, and preparing to counterattack, to charge, to pounce is
that deeply buried tiredness, that doesn't—and before you can finish
your sentence, before arriving at some conclusion, he asks, *Are you
in the habit of keeping a diary? Do you like recording your days and
nights?* So that's how you want to play it, is it? you murmur to yourself. So you'll follow hot on his heels. Both of you at a run. And talking more quickly than your normal speed, with pent-up intensity,
you'll race him, make him anxious, force him out of the nirvana
and Zen besetting him, and you'll say to him, *No I don't keep a
diary. No. Why would I? Everyone keeps one now. Relatives, girl-
friends, old schoolmates, work colleagues, and even neighbors,
lovers, whether passing or steady, those who turn against me, who
ignore me, who think of me or love me, strangers on the street, even
the dead, record time's passing, the motionless and steadfast undulation of the nether time. To what end, then, one more self-account
book? We're up to the ears in diaries of mourning, pleasure, war,
work, holidays, tedium, solitude, self-promotion, self-satisfaction, or
self-torment.* And in a voice at once relaxed, firm, unwavering and
yet unperturbed, as though you were shooting him at point-blank
range with a silencer, you continue, *Besides there are so many who
live as if things happen, in the way they happen, not in order to happen, but only in order to swell, to enlarge, to fill that polymorphous,
compulsive diary of daily life. Notepad, tape recorder, Facebook,
selfie, Twitter, Instagram. And what if there's a global hacking, an
evil ecumenical plot, and everything is lost, everything is vaporized?
Notes and footnotes, posts, comments and replies, uploaded photos
and self-portraits, clandestine inboxes, vitriolic tweets? If suddenly,*

that is, without warning, all their connections with social reality, whether apparent or concealed, were cut, how would they react? I'm curious. Will they burst into tears like little children who've had their toys taken from them? Will they start taking tranquilizers? Or will they see themselves as news heroes, information martyrs? And immediately afterward, you speak softly, almost in a whisper, as though someone were sleeping or gravely ill, though maybe deep down you want to alarm him, to make him miss words, lose your thread, and, why not, to feel that he's going deaf, losing control, getting old, and along with his hair and his virility is also losing his hearing. Even his relationship with time is—how can you put it? His voice, yes, his voice, sometimes sounds like that of a twenty-five-year-old, at others of a forty-year-old, even of a fifty-year-old. He's a today-tomorrow-yesterday type. All at the same time. That's why there are times when he breathes as though he's wrapped in swaddling clothes or lying naked in the coffin. Anyhow. And grunting something out, you say, *My days and nights hardly concern anyone, not even me. So what's the point of coming down with tendonitis and ruining my eyesight? Why should I try to save everything that does and doesn't happen to me? Everything I think, dream, crave so exhaustively that afterward I feel that not only have they happened to me in exactly the way I think of them, dream of them, and crave them, but that I've already cast them aside, tired of them, and rejected them. And I ask myself, really ask myself, who could possibly be interested in my tedious pursuits and my even more tedious thoughts? And that's not to mention that I'll never find a suitable hiding place to hoard away what I don't want to fall into anyone's hands. A burnt diary is an ideal diary. Only a diary in ashes saves you from excessive worry. And because for me to write something,*

anything at all, and then delete it straightaway is a little like my
wanting to empty the sea with a teaspoon, in other words to tear the
page into tiny pieces or, for even greater security, to burn the entire
diary so as to erase from the face of the earth that which, at the same
moment, I feel connects me with something that recalls me and with
something that distorts me, disguises me, erases me, pulverizes me,
that's why I allow time to slip through my hands, my hair, between
my legs. And all the while you're talking, you hear him sighing
deeply. As though someone were having trouble breathing, were
masturbating, were bored to tears, were ready to bang his head
against the wall. Because he does that too. Supposedly by chance,
supposedly by accident. He sighs, coughs, belches, blows his nose.
While you're talking. Not at all discreetly. It goes without saying.
Given that his aim is to discombobulate you. Which is why, deep-
ening your voice, imbuing it with hints of sarcasm, you say to him,
Of course I keep a diary. Unfailingly. It's a fact. I keep a record of
even the air that I breathe, of even the dust on my shoes. How can I
put it more frankly, more bluntly: what's not noted down doesn't
exist. There are times when I wonder whether I live just to scribble on
the pages in my diary. To fill them with sentences that are uncompro-
mising, panic-stricken, sentences that coil around themselves like
snakes or snap like ropes in a sea storm, but also with words that are
ignored, slandered, words that suffocate equally whether in dictio-
naries or out in the fresh air, words that feel under their skin that
reality is what cuts them off from what's real, words that want to
blow their brains out and words that want to be buried alive under
the ground; most of them, however, legions of words, want to stuff
themselves with silence, to seal their mouths, to no longer signify
what they signify, given that for so many frigging centuries they've

been signifying what they frigging signify, where's the good in it, where's the progress? Did it make anyone better? Was anyone saved from himself or from his neighbor? If anyone has ever felt more replete, more self-sufficient, more serene after coming out with precise or pithy words, let him raise his hand. A forest of no hands. That's all I see. Better that they no longer signify anything. Let their meanings take a hike. Begone with them! Nothing, begone! So that you say "dog" and you mean "I'm thirsty," you say "that's unbearable" and you mean "that's my island," you say "I'll love you forever" and mean "dead for a day." And it's then that I start up a conversation with the woman I wake up with, have breakfast with, use the bathroom with (we often scrub each other's backs, one of us with a soft sponge and special soap for allergies), get dressed with, get into the car with, arrive at work with, return home with (both of us done-in, exhausted), shop with (organic the one, special offers the other) at the supermarket, eat something light with (sometimes the one has an appetite for something more spicy and the other is unhappy about it), watch, without watching, the news with, get ill with (the one hale and hearty, the other sickly), talk (to others) with over the telephone, cry with (couldn't be more different), fart with, masturbate with (we often come together), meet friends with, make love with (the one leaning toward wistful toy boys, the other toward smiling old crocks), go to the movies, plays (constantly disagreeing on what to see), and bars with, get drunk with, throw up with, travel with, get bored with, think about committing suicide with (the one with sleeping pills, the other by drowning), go to sleep with (the one sleeping like a log, the other like an owl), and all this to what end? And in unison, a duet, we ask, What lasts longer? The moment that you note down, that you photograph, sing, and dance or the moment that you let pass, be

*born, live, and die as a moment, with its own negligible or overpower-
ing weight?* And before you can finish your last word or take a
breath, he asks you, *When you start something, do you usually finish
it or not?* No breath for him, no breath for you. *Usually,* you say to
him, *I leave everything half-finished. Half-finished books, half-
finished relationships, half-finished meals, half-finished sentences,
half-finished vacations. Do I do what I am? Am I what I do? Whatever the case, I feel half-finished. I am half-finished. I'm surrounded
by the loose ends of things and words. That feeling that nothing finishes, since nothing finishes for good, given that what you leave in
the middle you can take up again exactly where you left it, even start
it again from the beginning, because perhaps this time, without any
more postponement, without fail, you might see it through to the
end, have done with him. This vagueness pleasantly disconcerts me.
It almost moves me. That rocking back and forth in time makes me
feel free. As if I were breathing mountain air. Filling my lungs, my
head, my blood with something fresh. Unpolluted. Don't give me a
deadline. You kill me like that. Don't divide my time into pieces. Of
course, everyone wants reliable pupils, reliable workers, reliable
voters and taxpayers, they need them. They're the foundation, the
backbone, the model for society. They are society's critical mass.
Once I was perplexed, worried, angry at not being one of them. That
I wasn't a piece of the norm's effective, advantageous puzzle. I lived
at odds with myself. I felt useless. I became part of the fringe of my
own volition. Whereas time was time inside me, outside it was something else, something that froze and enflamed me. Indiscriminately.
And in contrast to those, consistent with the effective, advantageous
puzzle, I perceived time outside as being shriveled, numb. That's why
I reacted, that's why I was annoyed, that's why I cut myself off, so as*

not to become time outside. So as not to become like his mug. And shall I tell you something else? Just between us, I can accept the one who finishes earlier, completes what he's undertaken before the deadline ends, before the bell goes. I can accept him. He has his little fad. He's stressed, highly responsible, consistent, though with something gnawing at him, in his inner time. The one who is unnerved at the thought of being an hour, a day overdue is outside my visual frame. I don't see him. Or rather I see him, but I find him so dislikable that it's as though I don't see him. I believe that. No, really, I believe it. I'm not saying it just to say something. Punctuality is an incurable illness. It can't be treated either by years of psychotherapy or by psychotropic drugs and repeated electroshock. I know, I know what they say, only too well, I know, about me personally and about all those like me, about all we who are redundant and self-effacing. One moment unsatisfied, the next irresponsible. In fact, there are those who'll have you lie down on the analyst's couch and, in a low and profound voice, say to you, "You're looking for your father, your teacher, someone to set limits for you." Listen, I don't know about the others, but personally I've had enough. I've even been called a wacky perfectionist. And a somber idealist. I'd like to know where they think these things up. Unless they don't think them up but pinch them from some book or other. There's only one thing they haven't thought to say something about. Not a word. Not even a hint. About everything else they've said plenty. All the secondary things, the insignificant and inconsequential. Because if they were to say something about this, I'd listen. There's some point to it. The only observation that has any meaning. Call it an abjection, call it a reproach, call it what you will. When you're afraid of finishing something, when you suffocate in the time limits imposed by a certain date, when you pro-

crastinate with tangible or intangible excuses, when you want time to contract and expand according to your own mood, your own endurance, then it touches you with its wax hand. You know it, you don't know it. You realize it, you don't realize it. Then, at the back of your mind, in your soul's attic, something starts to flash. I agree. Something wanes flashing on and off. But no one has said that. And tell me, all you zealots of punctuality who sit us down and admonish us, reproach us, accuse us, consider us bad examples, point your finger at us who are gauche, left-handed in both hands, female cripples of time's limits, tell me, with hand on your heart, on your kidneys, on your balls, on your brow, wherever you want, when you finish something at the right time, neither before it's ripe nor after it's overmature, but at the right time, when you're super-precise, behind the collective praise, beneath the personal satisfaction, have you never felt a hand tapping you on the shoulder somewhat heavily? Touching you on the back of your neck so that you feel you're being touched by a snowman? And suddenly, as if something in your answer causes him anguish or as if he takes it personally as an indirect, direct, or open warning, though he is beyond reliability and unreliability, is unaccountable and has the right to unaccountability, whatever the case, he interrupts you and asks, *Do you consider yourself to be stable, unstable, or unclassifiable in your love life?* And on the one hand you wonder how to answer and on the other, what exactly he wants to know with this question. Given that you know, you're almost certain, that he's totally indifferent to your love life, whether you're married or divorced, whether you've been with ten men or a thousand. No, it's not personal. He's not focusing on you. It concerns all the women that he chooses to ask. Because, and there's an asterisk here, on his questionnaire, in his statistical field, in his interrogative framework, in his compulsive obsession, there's room only for women. From fresh young girls, through verified adults, students, unemployed, part-time and working women who want to fatten their purse, immigrant women without a roof over their heads, young mothers, dynamic professionals, but also women who don't work, who have their own means, who don't lack the money to fill their days, to old women, ailing, incapacitated, ready to give up the ghost. However, you're certain that, if it were possible, if there were no consequences, if he could, he would also question little girls and dead women. And that's not just hot air. Given that he often behaves to you, as verified adults and incontestably alive, as if you were little girls or long gone. On the one hand he wants you submissive, tame, malleable, and on the other, negative, tough, rebellious. He gets angry, without showing it, becomes annoyed, always obliquely, when you behave in the image and likeness of his wishes. Like how it is when someone pushes a door and you're at the other side and know that you mustn't give way immediately, so that it seems farcical, but neither must you put a wardrobe behind it so that the other one will be still pushing in the next life. In the end the only constant, nonnegotiable, unmovable point is the labyrinth of his ear. His eardrum can't endure contralto, mezzo-soprano, or soprano. For the bases, baritones, tenors, and countertenors he stuffs his ears with paper, cotton wool, or earplugs. He has no interest in the male gaze or the male touch. Or he has so great an interest, so deep and constant an interest, that he pelts it with stones, ostracizes it, throws it out of his present, his self-image, out of the narrative of his present and his self-image. Eventually, however, you grow tired of coming out with the same old song, and in answer to what he asked, you say to him, *There are times and times. There are* times when I suffer minor strokes. Continuous, mild. That's how I recall fleeting love affairs. The ones I experience quietly, discreetly, secretly, during long-standing relationships. I flirt and am flirted with. I let myself go. I might go with anyone. But no farther. I avoid those who might trouble or upset me. I keep well away from those kind. I can smell them. Just by looking at them. It's enough. Just a few words from them. More than enough. I only get involved with the ones I can handle. As soon as I see someone who's difficult or demanding—the knife's out. I cut all ties. I've no wish to get myself done in. To fall in love and then? Remain alone? I can't stand to be alone. Better a relationship that drags than to talk to the walls and be stuck to the phone. I'm fearful of women who go on vacation on their own. And those who foist themselves on friends at festive times. The halo of a lonely existence gives me migraine. All those former wives, former mothers, former professionals. They wear me out. Those women who work out a lot, read a lot, travel a lot, have the answer ready even before you ask them the question. They scare me stiff. The women who don't have a minute to spare, always have to be somewhere and always have someone waiting for them. Pilates, pottery classes, reading groups, environmental pursuits, walking clubs, voluntary work for refugees. Lest they find themselves with a bit of time, lest they find themselves face to face with and bump into their naked selves. Which is why all that time wasting and gadding about is really neither time wasting nor gadding, but rather airbags, multiple airbags that open after any collision with life in order to protect them, so they won't be shattered, won't be smashed to smithereens together with their beneficial time wasting, their creative gadding. But there are also times when I can't bear the dignified quagmire. I feel suffocated being with a man and thinking of another, doing a job that suffocates me, mixing with superficial friends who suffocate me, all the well-known causes of suffocation. In a word or two, confronting with humor, a modicum of sadness, and acquiescence all the things that don't brook humor, a modicum of sadness, and acquiescence. Then I become one of Chekhov's raging heroines. Masa with the ax. And I start hacking and hacking myself. At other times, when I was younger, when I'd left home, though maybe I wasn't so young and hadn't left home but was simply living there like someone already gone, like an absentee, living as though I lived miles away, so then, when I didn't know where I was and where I wasn't, whether I was twenty, thirty, or forty, I used to go with various men. On trains, at parties, on the beach, in the bathroom, in parking lots. Anywhere. I was addicted. With anyone at all. With drifters, adventurers, deadbeats. Given that if I knew anyone well enough to exchange a word with him, I wouldn't go near him. And although that baring of my sex wasted me, that skinning, the chase, the clandestine, the somnambulistic, I didn't drag myself away, remained glued, though it led me burning into a dead end. There. Again and again. Because whenever I closed my mouth around the penis of young, middle-aged, or aging males, men I didn't know, who I would never see again, one-night stands, a night more night than all the nights, a moment of drunkenness or despair, I felt as though I were suckling on my father's finger, licking my brother's nipple, swallowing the spittle from an anxious cousin's kiss. Fine, someone might wonder, did that tongue-wagger only ever swallow broken glass? Did she never know times of erotic insouciance and fulfillment? And before you have time to reply to your inner objection, to your silent soliloquy, before you can say that the moments when you shared sleep, dreams, and horniness with someone—in other words, the moments when you exchanged stories, in and out of sleep, in and out of horniness—disappeared, scattered like pepper, he asks you, *Have you ever thought that you might, it's not at all unlikely, be arrested for something that doesn't have the slightest thing to do with you, that you might be linked to something criminal, to something you haven't done?* And because no question is random or innocent, just to say something, just to pass the time, and so forth, you'll answer with a question, or, more precisely, you'll ask yourself out loud, *That I haven't done or that I think about so much that it's as though I've done it? Because when something is on your mind continuously, persistently, and for a long time, when you go to sleep and wake up with it, it's almost as though you've already done it. You feel a bit like those people who move objects using their thought or bend spoons and forks just by looking at them. Without even trying. As if it were something beyond them. And, naturally, there are always all those things that intrude, that intervene, that I do in my sleep or that run through my mind, without my being aware, perhaps not even caring in the end whether they are reprehensible or culpable. If, that is, in some part of the world, in some procedural system, some courts, judges and jurors, condemn, hand out the severest sentences, lead in chains to maximum-security prisons all those who in their sleep commit improprieties, even perform violent and criminal acts. Since this category of the guilty-innocent wishes, prays, and takes refuge in the most elaborate curses, the most secret concoctions, so that all the evils of the world might fall upon those who harmed them, injured them, or hurt them. And then we see that, just as there are crimes without punishment for various reasons, so also there are punishments without crimes for somewhat similar or other reasons. In fact, I often get confused, become disoriented, don't know which way I'm facing. Am I an offender or do I punish myself? Perhaps I punish my-self because, deep down, I have an offender's constitution? Or the opposite: in other words, I'm an offender because I like to punish myself?* And, *Whether offender or self-punisher,* he asks you, *do you prefer walking in the countryside or in the town?* And if you tell him that you don't like hiking, walking, going back and forth, whether on asphalt or earth, whether among apartment blocks or among trees. How will he take it? Neither urban scenes nor rural scenes. Will he be annoyed? That you like, get off on, dig sitting ensconced in some place, regardless of whether it's the noisiest spot in the world or the most secluded. Sitting and observing. Or not observing. Just sitting. Or even standing. Maybe even lying. Not remembering or forgetting. And not thinking. But not thinking, *Now I'm not thinking.* Just emptying yourself. Having a clear-out. With deft hand movements removing from your chest mud and straw, and from your groin mud, manure, and straw. Because you know. You know only too well. Whether you answer or don't answer, it's all the same. You're slow in accepting it, swallowing it, realizing it, but it happens. He doesn't feel annoyed, doesn't feel happy, doesn't feel disappointed, doesn't feel enthusiastic, doesn't feel flirtatious, and he doesn't underestimate, doesn't overestimate, doesn't condemn. A persistent, soul-destroying, lifelong doesn't. That's what it is. A questioning machine. And a questioning machine can only be op-posed by an answering machine. Which is why all you do is answer. You become entirely an answer. You avoid becoming part of the ob-session, you don't get involved in the business. What's he trying to pry out of you with that question? Is there any logic, coherence, strategy in his questionnaire? Is he asking you in order to get close to you, enlighten you, grope you, get under your skin, ridicule you, or annihilate you? Is he asking to clarify something or to obscure it? Is he asking for the thrill of the question or the fullness of the answer? Is he asking because he can no longer bear the loneliness or the silence? Is he asking because someone is holding a gun to his head? You put it all aside. And you answer. You become a callous respondent, a cold murderer of his questions. You answer. Gun, knife, poison, noose. You answer. Don't let there be any unanswered question. You answer. There won't be. Ever. You answer. Till he's out of questions. Till you've stuffed his mouth with answers. You answer. Even answers without questions. What will happen if you start to answer without a question? If, to put it differently, the answer precedes the question, so that the answer gives rise to the formulation of the question? It excites you just to think of him in that position. A former respondent, you answer and seek the question. Calmly and patiently, waiting for the question to your answer. He, the life-long questioner, will now come after. From now on he'll be the one doing the running, and he'll never get to the end. On the other hand you reflect that your relationship often opens into something beyond questions and answers. You often have the feeling, you believe, that the one thing he doesn't do is ask. Just like you. Because the things you say, more often than not, are anything but answers to his questions. More specifically, what would he ask you, what question would you elicit from him if you were to say to him, *I don't remember who told me, or what the one who told me was like, that in order to seduce someone I should act indifferent — in other words not make a show of ignoring him but neither concern myself overmuch with him.* Something else. *I don't recall what year it was that summer when I was on holiday and I had no mood either for swimming or for drinking or for flirting or for talking to anyone, and I spent* almost two months under an old mulberry tree smoking and listening all day long to a torn flag flapping against its rusty pole and all night, every night, just before daybreak, always just before daybreak, listening to a telephone in some neighboring house ringing continually with no one ever picking it up. No one. And something else. Once I was sitting at a bus stop. I can't even recall whether I was sitting there, on the metal bench under the shelter, because I was tired or disappointed, because it was raining, or because I was waiting for a bus. Did I live somewhere close by? Did I have some job to do around there? I've erased everything. What I haven't erased, however, is that sitting beside me on that metal bench at the bus stop were two men. As if they'd been sitting there forever. "I'll see you later," one said suddenly to the other, but without getting up to leave. "It's later now," said the other, after a long pause, without so much as looking at him. One was wearing a leather jacket and a red jockey cap, and the other a denim jacket and a yellow jockey cap. I don't imagine you want me to remember who was wearing what and who said what. Something more. "As soon as you sit at a table with acquaintances, friends, or colleagues," he said to me, "look around to find the one who's unfortunate, unprotected, vulnerable, the usual victim. If you can't find him? Start running. Without saying anything, without asking anything. Leave, just as you are. With the food in your mouth, the glass in your hand, with the napkin tied round your neck. You'll seem rude? Then seem rude. They won't invite you again? As if you would ever go again." She was sitting beside me at a long worktable. She started to talk to me without looking at me, without looking at anyone, while, dexterously, she was slowly cutting half an egg, an olive, half a tomato, a piece of cheese, food which, however, she never put in her mouth. Suddenly, she pushed her chair back and started to run. But by mistake, she headed toward the washroom. With the result that, flushed and excited because of her untimely flight, she this time bolted toward the exit, forgetting, in her haste, her scarf, a mauve silk scarf that smelled of sweet mustiness. Something more. I don't recall how either the mother or the child were, or even the park where the mother was shouting to the child, sometimes "Go far nearby" and sometimes "Come close away." Something more. Some secondhand days, with a secondhand mood, I roam around the secondhand city where I live, and following secondhand routes, I see secondhand images, hear secondhand sounds, am surprised by secondhand scenes on the street, while at times I'm under a secondhand cloudbank and at others a secondhand clear sky, meet secondhand strangers, secondhand friends, observe secondhand men that I like, use secondhand words to describe secondhand thoughts or take refuge in a secondhand silence in order to escape all those secondhand secondhands that inundate me, seeing that, as my secondhand walk continues, the only thing that has any meaning for me, a meaning that's less secondhand, is for me to walk aimlessly, but without showing it, without shouting it from the rooftops, for me to walk as if I were going at a secondhand speed, with a secondhand mood, to keep a business or social appointment, and as my walk continues, I bump into, continually encounter secondhand violence or secondhand indifference, at every step, at every moment, and whenever, every so often, I come across something not secondhand, I feel that it's a secondhand statistical error or, in the best of cases, a secondhand simulation of something imperishable or spontaneous. Something more. I never want to see him again, never, not in this world or the next, if it exists, which it doesn't, though, sometimes, I think that not even this one here exists, the so-called real one, since it's not possible for things to go so badly, so disastrously, while we pretend to be indifferent, stupid, even unyielding, uncompromising, optimistic, resilient, continuing to believe that it exists, calling this walk life, a walk without beginning or end in a muddy landscape, in a muddy light, in a muddy time, and when our courage fails us, pinching ourselves so we might wake up from this prodigal walk, but the only thing we manage is to feel pain as we walk in even muddier mud. Something more. I possess inexhaustible deposits of discontent, negativity, discouragement, huge secret reservoirs of ineptitude, failure, frustration, labyrinthine conduits of weariness, weariness, weariness, scattered throughout the length and breadth of the world, for every eventuality. Consequently, don't hold out hope. Don't hold out hope of encouraging me in anything, of supporting me in the slightest, of persuading me to see things differently, with acquiescence or compassion, of discussing with me, of negotiating with me what I can already see, inside me and outside, what I see with eyes open or closed. So leave me alone to tie that casual zero round my neck, to button up better my fishbone emptiness and to continue, if what I'm continuing can be continued, if the word continue continues to have any meaning, but how else can you call what doesn't stop, what never ceases, what continues even when you are motionless somewhere, rooted to the spot, as if nailed down, as if planted? Something more. I'm usually scared of the nights and shy of the days. I can say this, substantiate it. It happens. It happens. But not always. There are times when I don't feel I'm so disappointed, that is, essentially, fundamentally, unyieldingly disappointed, so as to be scared of the nights and shy of the days. No, I'm not. With the result that I doubt. Because if I were, if, that is, I were essentially, fundamentally, unyieldingly disappointed, I'd also be scared of the not-nights, shy of the not-days. Something which isn't the case. No, it's not the case. That's not the case. And something else that isn't the case is that I don't remember if what I just said is something I've thought, I've heard, I've read, or I've dreamt. And that's annoying, very annoying, not to say unpleasant or insufferable. Because all this, I don't know how to put it, I don't even know if there's a way of saying it somehow, expands into a series of things. It spreads like a virus to more and more things. It infects almost everything I think, hear, read, or dream. And is it possible to go on living if you stop thinking, hearing, reading, or dreaming? Is it? Of course it's not. Just as it's not possible to cease thinking, hearing, reading, and dreaming, lest everything inside you get confused, mixed up, become tangled, and afterward just try distinguishing what it is you think and think it, what it is you hear and hear it, what it is you read and read it, what it is you dream and dream it. Something more. There are some days when I feel missing, I feel that I'm a missing person, one who was lost, forgotten, or perhaps one who pretends to be lost or distracted in order to escape from something, to slip away from something that she can't exactly define, with the result that she wanders aimlessly for a long time in various places, some familiar, some unfamiliar, some neither familiar nor unfamiliar, until eventually she decides, without knowing even herself what exactly it is she decides, in other words she's ignorant not only of the depth but also of the surface of her decision, to have recourse to the authorities and report her disappearance. But the moment she appears before the sergeant on night duty at the police station, filthy as she is, disheveled, tired, and hungry, and begins relating to him and explaining what happened and how it happened, unable naturally to tell him why what happened happened, he bursts out laughing, into uncontrollable laughter, is unable even to keep up pretenses, as with tears in his eyes he calls to his colleagues, even releasing the detainees from the cells, and gesticulating madly beckons to passersby on the street, so that all together they might hear the funny, side-splitting, ludicrous story of a missing woman whose disappearance no one had reported, for whom no one was looking, about whom there was no announcement in the newspapers, for whose discovery no reward had been offered, till the actual victim herself had decided that she was no longer missing and with a dreary vagueness, which nevertheless provokes waves of uncontrollable laughter, came to the police to verify what was unknown to anyone, of no interest to anyone, of no concern to anyone. Something more. You drink a glass of water, a glass of wine, a glass of beer, and you're not there, you eat a sandwich, a piece of cake, some fruit, and you're not there, you walk under a flowering bower in the rain, through a foggy landscape, in a burnt forest, and you're not there, you dance with a man who adores you, and you're not there, you play with the children of your best friend, and you're not there, you cry, laugh, become angry at something you remember, and you're not there, you travel by train, plane, boat, and you're not there, you fall silent, and you're not there. Do you want more details? Aren't these bits and pieces enough for you? Don't they verify, prove, validate the fact that I'm always, I'll always be where I'm not? Something more. The words oldie and new awaken something inside me—they're unbearable. Oldie, that is, cracks, tarnish, wear, fray, chinks, patches, damp. Horrid. And new, that is, shiny, untouched, unused, strong smell of materials, with a guarantee and spares, straight from the box, as they say. Doubly horrid. I don't know which of the two is worse. The so-called old year, which expires, snuffs it, breathes its last, or the so-called new year,

which swims in mucus, does nothing but cry and crap, that unbearable weakness that eats you alive if you don't take care of it, if you
don't love it? Something more. I don't recall where I was sleeping
and when I opened my eyes I saw her sitting on my bed, nor that she
had thin lips and a large forehead. My memory completely erased
how for a long time she gazed at me calmly, stared at me without the
slightest trace of indiscretion, and when eventually I told her in a
sleepy voice, though with displeasure simmering deep down, "I know
very well who you are," then she, not sharply, softly, very softly, as
though in a dreamy mood, said, "Fine, then introductions are un-
necessary," and, as she got up to go out of my bedroom, brushing
aside her dirty white wings, she added, "Your problem is that you
don't need anyone at your side." Something more. I don't recall
where I was, in what city I was idling or feeling bored stiff, when I
saw in the street a man as thin as a crack, with two enormous, velvety
sorrowful eyes, eyes like those of a horse, so big they were, groping in
the air, waving his hands as if he were feeling something very tangible, very close, very dear, which is probably why his eyes were wet
and shiny, his horse-like eyes shone like lakes in the light of dusk.
Something more. Nor do I recall his appearance or his build; all I
recall is that, when he entered the bar in which I was already on my
third bourbon, a deserted joint with good booze where I went when I
wanted to drink as if I were drinking alone at home, before he even
downed his undiluted vodka, he turned out the pockets of his trousers
and coat, methodically and deftly, as if he had done it many times
before, and from his frayed pockets took a humming top, a little
battery-powered fan, a child's sock with a hole in it, a red stone, pips
from an unknown fruit, not necessarily in that order, and other small
objects, which he pulled out of his pockets as though they were

unique finds and, after taking them out, arrayed them on the counter like toy soldiers, then while paying for the three vodkas he had already downed like water and gathering together his choice junk, he said to me and the barman, as if addressing eternity, "So how do you see things? As crazy or eternal?" And these words sounded somewhat hollow and out of place given that the bar was as empty as a cenotaph, the barman was dozing over the cash register, and I myself had for some time been seeing only a blur. Something more? Enough. That's why you just answer. You answer. To questions that are indifferent, provocative, fiendish. Not to jumble things or to go on too much. To questions that thirst for answers or crave to be transformed into other questions. You answer. Even to hints of questions, to questions before they even break out of their shell, before they even become questions. Because if you don't answer, if you don't give an answer, you enter the burrow of the mole. The subterranean, labyrinthine home of the dormouse. And try getting out afterward. And suddenly, as though he were circulating in your head, naked, unwashed, abandoned, but maybe also spruced up, dressed to the nines, with a brandy in his hand and a cigar in his mouth, he asks you, *I don't remember whether I've already asked you, do you have dreams about animals?* Of course, he's asked already, and of course he remembers that he's already asked you. Given that it's a common secret, there are no longer any questions that haven't been asked or answers that haven't been given. Which is why you want to tell him, to tell him again and again, to repeat in identical fashion or slightly modified, what you had told him two weeks before, three months before, a year before — even you've lost count — that recently you've been having dreams almost exclusively about animals. Which is why it no longer surprises you at all that bears are crying in your cupboards, beheaded hens are running on your balcony, vultures are snoring on your bed, snakes are suckling on your breast, mice are falling about laughing while keeping you company and watching comedies on television. Though of late the situation has grown worse; hybrid animals, not the most pleasant crosses of the fauna you meet, usually on various forms of transport, on constant trips, ineffectual ones, comically ineffectual ones, have started burrowing into your pillow. And while you're getting ready to tell him about that train, the ticket for which you can't find at the last minute, though so much the better, as that high-speed express was carrying, instead of passengers, enormous shiny cockroaches adorned with the colored plumage of parrots, or about that ship, that inexplicably empty ship, on which everyone from the captain down to the cabin boy had the face of an anteater, the limbs of an ape, and the tail of a crocodile, he interrupts you, for no obvious reason, and with his smooth voice, his icy tone, as if you were listening to someone absent opening and closing his lips, articulating words, forming sentences, he asks you, *When you're sad, do you shut yourself away or do you open yourself up to people?* And while you reflect, think, and wonder at what he'll do with so many scraps of stories, so many odds and ends of recollections, so many remnants of dreams, so many remains of incoherent animals, you attune yourself to his spineless, lifeless tonality, and you say to him, *One year, when in the space of a week I'd lost two of my best friends to cancer and on top of that I'd ended a long-standing difficult relationship, inconsolable as I was, recently deceased, sorry, recently separated I meant, I was walking a thin psychological line, on the edge of numerous things, I couldn't bear for a moment to be inside, as though the house were throwing me out, as though someone had set* fire to me and I went off like a madwoman, ate whatever junk I found, slept in cheap hotels, started up conversations with strangers, in short, I was beset by a mania for being out, and I saw the streets, the squares, and the arcades, the underground passageways as corridors and niches in my house, which is why I gulped, drank down the passersby like matured years-old distillation, as though the unknown crowd wasn't unknown but was a crowd of old schoolfriends, deceased relatives, or unfulfilled loves, and after a while, after some days, I turned the lining of my craze inside out and was gripped by another craze, the craze for inside, the craze of the hermit, the recluse, outside the ground gave way beneath my feet, I would forget my name, could no longer endure even my own shadow. Which is why I changed my landline, turned off my cell phone, logged off Facebook, and no longer opened the door to anyone. Only to home delivery. Given that all day long I was inside, incarcerated, behind closed shutters, eating pizza, Chinese, and kebabs, watching only old romantic movies and comedies, unable to bear either the news bulletins or discussions or anything else, which is why my head, from all the laughter and kisses, had become like polystyrene. So during that period of my alternating craze for inside and outside, whenever I leaned toward my mania for running for dear life, as soon as I saw a miserable little bar or a lonely tavern, I'd sit down there. I drank and ate at my leisure, as though I were waiting for an old forgotten friend. In the end I'd start chatting to the owner, we'd drink together, become stinking drunk by closing time, since evidently this unknown, morose, abandoned guy, swatting flies behind the counter or the food cabinet, is the old, forgotten friend I was waiting for. And so the time passed, which is the only thing that drone knows how to do, that scoundrel, that frowsty smell, that piece of shit, what else can I *call it, and some days I felt imprisoned, erasing the fact that I was self-imprisoned, that no one was preventing me from going outside, though there are times when no guard is more disagreeable, more unpredictable, not to say more frightening, than the particular one, the one you have before you, because you hate him, want to gouge his eyes out, but at least you know who he is, you know who put him there, whose designs he's serving, anyhow, this story with the visible and concealed guard is so old and confused, whichever way you look at it, which is why I put it aside and stuck my ear to the wall to listen to nothing, the yawning, the groaning, the farting, the laughing, the whispering, the cursing, the music score of the dividing wall, while a few days later I took to crawling the streets, wandered aimlessly around like a dog with its tail between its legs, like a cat on hot bricks, hoping to leave behind me that wretched body, that wretched body with the stupid smile that was me, hoping to work up the courage to get carried away, or at least the rashness, given that my courage never for one moment remained fixed but was ever fidgeting this way and that, hoping to branch out, become attuned with the solitary polyphony of the crowd, hoping that at some moment I might become the broken, fragmented, atonal melody of everyone, of no one.* And while, as an aura, as an echo, you're still outside in the world, in the human, dizzy, colorful anthill, at the same moment that you of course are still motionless and alone in bed, on a deserted beach, or in your stationary car, he asks you, *What things annoy you more? Straight out, as they come to you, you don't need to order them according to the degree of displeasure.* And then, as though being long attuned to his fading timbre, you begin pell-mell with your long spiel, about those who squash empty plastic bottles, those who bite their nails, those who talk with their mouths full, those who wear slippers at home, those who avoid the eyes of others in the elevator, those who extend their hands to you listlessly and expect from you a warm handshake and even more, those who, having lost the demarcation line between the private and the public, speak in a loud voice, seeking an audience anywhere, those who slam the doors behind them, but also those who close the door noiselessly like ghosts, those who, while not knowing a foreign language well, speak with an accent as though they knew it backward, those who while cooking continually lick their fingers, wanting to show that what they are cooking is so delicious, those who clean their teeth using their fingers, those who fish with dynamite or eat fry, the vegetarians who torture people, the animal lovers who behave to animals as if they were humans, the artists who pretend to be above money and self-projection, and who flay you alive if they feel wronged by you, the authorities on any subject, those who fall silent in order to feign profundity or suffering, those who, while up to their necks in compromises in their own personal lives, outwardly propose drastic measures and daring moves, always when it comes to others' lives, those who feel fantastic with their bodies, their ideas, their jobs and so forth, those who in bed are like a parody of a porno star, and also the women who smell their hair, the men who smell their socks, the kids who laugh like their parents, the women who live with closeted gays in the name of companionship, the men who turn round in the street to see whether anyone is looking at them, the kids who immediately assume familiarity, the *burnt roses*, in other words, the women who live, read, interpret emotionally everything around them, the men—and though you could tell him, enumerate for him, unravel till kingdom come everything that annoys you, could grow old with this question alone, to the degree that what doesn't bother you, compared with what does bother you, is just a drop in the ocean, you stop given that he begins to cough protractedly. Curbing tactics. Short pause, little cough, long pause, a succession of little coughs, and then he says to you, *Tell me, is there some story that you haven't experienced yourself, that isn't yours, but that you feel so much a part of you that it's as if you'd experienced it, which is why when you relate it, you relate it as if it were yours?* You're expecting this question. It's pestering him. It's smoldering inside him. But before you say anything, you want to clarify something. For yourself, not for him. Probably not even for yourself. About the stories. When you relate a story, when you end a story, many stories end, if they end, at the same time. Contiguous, competitive, counterbalancing ones. First of all, the story plot, what the story's about and of course who's relating it, how you relate it. Despondently, with zest, as a task, enchanted. Undoubtedly, when a story ends, it's like releasing all the other stories that you left aside to devote yourself to the story that you finally chose to relate, to tell. Afterward, you reflect, is the story that you've just related a one-off story, or is it connected to some previous stories that you've already related? And how will it intersect, if it intersects, with stories that you'll relate in the future? And is it certain that this story, related in this way, is meaningful for someone? Finally—the story's story, the story that carries along all stories—will there be a story to follow? Will you be able to tell a story again? To relate something without there being a specific reason, without someone asking you? That's all. And you come back to the story of the questions, to what he asked you, to his question. To begin with, it's a self-question. If we accept that there are some which aren't. But in this case, it cries out, it's staring you in the face.

I balk at asking myself, so I ask you. A reply through a representative. I take your hand and plunge it where I'm afraid to plunge my own. Very convenient, no doubt. But for you it's not easy. Not at all. You're pushed to even relate your own stories as your own. How can you not see as a concession that constant tell, tell all the time. Not relating an unfamiliar story, someone else's story as your own. And saying it in a way that he won't become bored, annoyed, dismayed, shocked. I've said it before. He's fucked us up with all his not and not. And not only that. Every time, you dig deep, turn the world upside down, rack your brains, wring even your soul to find what? What hasn't been said? A needle in a haystack. Something less said, something said differently, something not said at all. On top of everything else he has a delicate stomach and can't bear reheated stories. And a sensitive skin, because he can't bear even the ones with heavy makeup. Above all, however, he has the memory of an elephant. He even remembers the dots. And your hanging question. A story already told is a spent story. Axiom. So for the time being you say to him, *We're sad, very sad. Whores are sad people. The ones who laugh about the money they make from whoring are just stupid. Cranks. Stupid whores. Aren't there stupid politicians? Cops? There are stupid politicians and there are stupid cops and there are stupid priests. I'm a whore. And it gets my blood up when they call me a prostitute or a hooker. I feel like gouging your eyes out when you see me as someone who earns money doing something she enjoys. I feel like smashing everything. I'm not a loose-liver either. I'm up to the ears in shit. And the only public service I perform is that I swim in your excrement. I didn't fall out of the sky. I chose the shit. My grandpa called me a dung beetle when he found out how I was living. Shit, no matter how you dress it up, remains shit. Even if you* empty a bucket of cologne over it, it still smells of shit. And nobody wants shit. Naturally. Only you when you come here and pay to eat it. Because I'm feeding you shit. Naturally. Because you're a shithead too. Given that you get it on with all this shit. You lie down in shit. You come in shit. You pay for this shit. You feel wonderful in the shit. What more natural? And then there's the other thing. How do you bear the other person's flesh inside you? Nothing more natural. But the worst of all are the kisses. Not the fondling, but the kisses. With my pussy you can do what you like. But what do you want with my mouth? Because there are those who insist on kissing you. When they kiss me I think of practical things. Bills, tax office, medical tests. Worrying things. That I'm ill. That my stomach's aching, that I have a fever and I'm throwing up. And so I throw up your kisses, your conversation, and your fucking soul. The only thing I don't throw up is your money. No, the kinky stuff isn't difficult. The kinky stuff is routine. That's what I'm paid for. If the other one didn't want kinky stuff, he'd sit at home. With his wife, his pecker, his little old mother. He wouldn't come to me, would he? Though some of the kinky stuff is downright amusing. Like those who fall in love with me and whisper sweet nothings to me. I had a judge who wept when I stuck my finger in his ass, called me mommy, and wanted me to suckle him like a baby. And afterward he went off to preside. And made decisions as to who was innocent and who guilty. I've had a lot like that. Respectable on the outside, losers on the inside. Naturally I hate all men. First of all, there are no men. Only customers. Nor are there any lovers. That's something that only the women who don't get laid or the kids who get off on porno believe. Not to mention that I rarely come now, and I've no appetite for sex. I hate them all from deep down inside. The leftists and rightists and the rich and the poor. And *the immigrants too. And those who drown them and those who rob them and those who beat them up. And the good-looking and the ugly. And those who swear and those who are self-effacing and polite. All of them. And the kids who are still at school and the potbellies. And those who can get it up and those who can't. And those who forget and those out of the shop window. And those who stare at you like sorrowful dogs and those who stare at you with creepy eyes. The sick ones. And those who want to fuck their mothers, sisters, daughters. All the ones who come here, I hate them all. And those who don't come here and treat their wives like whores, I despise them too. And their wives, who pride themselves on being treated like whores. I'm at odds with them too. It's one thing to be a whore and another to be like a whore.* And while you're telling him the story of an impassioned hooker, sorry, *whore*, of a bacchante, of a contemporary maenad, he interrupts you, politely it's true this time, to say to you, *The story you've just told me isn't unfamiliar to me. You've related it once before. Eighteen months, five days, and six and a half hours ago. Have you forgotten? Then the heroine was a misanthropic painter. Same plot, same tone of voice. Self-injury, desperation, brutality. Where the clients were art lovers or collectors, in keeping with their purse strings, and painting is prostituting, I prostitute my inner wares with colors.* And then he falls silent. Either you see him as a sleuth of novel stories or as a typical hypochondriac. He falls silent. Silence. Persistent. Not so long. Or menacing. No connection with his silences that are sudden like cloudbursts. Those that take hold of you and shake you. When you don't know whether something upset him, annoyed him, whether he went away, whether he left for good, even whether he died. The abundance of nothing. No. But neither the silence of serenity. The craving for concentration, the thirst for inertness. An emptying. Of questions and answers. Emptying. As though you were concentrating on a slight visible silence, barely perceptible. Molecular. Ambivalent. As if he were asking you to end it, to break it. To speak. To replace the previous story with another. Probably he's asking you to prolong his silence with your own. To allow the one silence to penetrate the other. No. Don't come out with any story. Neither a new one, nor an old one. He's asking you to come out with a story that's told with sealed lips and is heard with plugged ears. Not possible? It will be. Doesn't exist? You'll find it. Like him, when he asks, which is like he wasn't asking, and when he doesn't ask, as if he were asking. For you to enter into the closet of his silences. That's what he's asking you. To violate the privacy of his wardrobe. To rummage. To inhale. To listen. Above all. The silence of an elevator. The silence of a kiss. The silence after a terrorist hit or a terrible earthquake. The silence at the moment that we both come. The silence between words. The silence of the precipice. The silence of the persecuted. The silence between silences. Velvety, wooly, cotton, linen, silken, synthetic. Silences. To try on as many silences as you can. To wear them, combine them. And then, without a second thought, without giving hardly any thought, you blurt out a story to him, and you don't know whether he will take it the wrong way, whether it will annoy him, and you don't really care in the end, a story that you recall as something that hasn't happened to you and yet you bring it to mind as something very intense, virtually unforgettable, yet a story that's been experienced by some other woman in your place, a stranger, a woman unknown to you, one you've never met in your life, one who may very well be already dead, who experienced what she experienced as if you had experienced it, as if you were her cast, the ragdoll of all that the woman experienced, since it was as if you were experiencing it. It's her story that you tell him, the story of the woman you seemingly don't resemble, in either appearance or personality. But if you dig below the surface, you'll discover that, after all, you're identical, sister souls, inconceivably similar, ideal copies of each other, and isn't this precisely why you didn't decide to separate, to break up, to pretend from that moment to ignore each other's existence? Of course, the issue at this moment is purely practical. What has been exchanged between you, if it's been exchanged, and how it was exchanged may be of some interest but it's not urgent, not pressing. The crucial thing is who this story belongs to. Not on the level of rights, of possession, up to here it's mine and from then on it's yours, but on the level of concentration and peace. Yes. Because peace is always unique. Indivisible. Consubstantial. Solid. Not getting to the bottom of it, you begin and say to him, *"I'm not saying that," says the woman drinking coffee. "So if you're not saying that, what are you saying?" says the man drinking tea. "I'm saying how long are we going to go on telling stories?" says the woman drinking coffee, every so often biting her fleshy lips, as though annoyed at what she just came out with or thought of but didn't dare come out with. "Don't you like telling stories?" says the man drinking tea, every so often closing his eyes as though recalling something or falling asleep instantaneously. "I'm not sure," says the woman drinking coffee, every so often biting her fleshy lips, as though annoyed at what she just came out with or thought of but didn't dare come out with, the woman who is engrossed in the hands of the man drinking tea, long, bony fingers, dotted with blotches. "Why?" says the man drinking tea, every so often closing his eyes as though recalling something or falling asleep instantaneously, and through closed eyelids he sees, almost fondles, the sinewy, well-shaped legs of the woman drinking coffee. "Because sometimes I feel that the things we say both are and aren't stories," says the woman drinking coffee, every so often biting her fleshy lips, as though annoyed at what she just came out with or thought of but didn't dare come out with, the woman who at times is engrossed in the hands of the man drinking tea, long, bony fingers, dotted with blotches, and at others in a tardiness that permeates his movements and not just these, but also his thinking. "A story can be anything," says the man drinking tea, every so often closing his eyes as though recalling something or falling asleep instantaneously, and through closed eyelids he sees, almost fondles, the sinewy, well-shaped legs of the woman drinking coffee, the woman whose profile reminds him of his mother and whose face reminds him of some woman he was passionately in love with and whom he's been trying to get out of his mind for years now. "That frightens me even more," says the woman drinking coffee, every so often biting her fleshy lips, as though annoyed at what she just came out with or thought of but didn't dare come out with, the woman who at times is engrossed in the hands of the man drinking tea, long, bony fingers, dotted with blotches, and at others in a tardiness that permeates his movements and not just these, but also his thinking, even with the tempo of his voice. "Don't let it drive you crazy," says the man drinking tea, every so often closing his eyes as though recalling something or falling asleep instantaneously, and through closed eyelids he sees, almost fondles, the sinewy, well-shaped legs of the woman drinking coffee, the woman whose profile reminds him of his mother and whose face reminds him of some woman he was passionately in love with whom he's been trying to get out of his mind for years now, though every so often getting confused, as he feels that the face of the woman drink-*

ing coffee reminds him of his mother and her profile of the woman he was passionately in love with whom still today he can't forget or even alleviate the weight of her memory. "Then there are times when I become worried or bored when I don't have anything to say. At other times I feel that someone is dictating to us what we say. And at times he's listening to what we say. He listens, orders, records, twists, and conveys it as he wishes to the traffickers of stories. Tell me something, do traffickers of stories exist?" says the woman drinking coffee, every so often biting her fleshy lips, as though annoyed at what she just came out with or thought of but didn't dare come out with, the woman who at times is engrossed in the hands of the man drinking tea, long, bony fingers, dotted with blotches, and at others in a tardiness that permeates his movements and not just these, but also his thinking, even with the tempo of his voice, though without him having any problem of inflexibility or dullness or psychological transfixion. "Don't let it drive you crazy. Nothing exists," says the man drinking tea, every so often closing his eyes as though recalling something or falling asleep instantaneously, and through closed eyelids he sees, almost fondles, the sinewy, well-shaped legs of the woman drinking coffee, the woman whose profile reminds him of his mother and whose face reminds him of some woman he was passionately in love with whom he's been trying to get out of his mind for years now, though every so often getting confused, as he feels that the face of the woman drinking coffee reminds him of his mother and her profile of the woman he was passionately in love with whom still today he can't forget or even alleviate the weight of her memory, though again without being a hundred percent sure, given that his mother stubbornly refused to have her photo taken full face and would only be photographed in profile. "Don't tell me again not to *let it drive me crazy. That drives me even more crazy," says the woman drinking coffee, every so often biting her fleshy lips, as though annoyed at what she just came out with or thought of but didn't dare come out with, the woman who at times is engrossed in the hands of the man drinking tea, long, bony fingers, dotted with blotches, and at others in a tardiness that permeates his movements and not just these, but also his thinking, even with the tempo of his voice, though without him having any problem of inflexibility or dullness or psychological transfixion, but it's more a sense of resignation, an aura of inertia that surrounds him, insufferably recalling that light sensation of falling, but never once and for all, rather a constant fa-a-a-l-ling of being that bared the days and nights of her father. "Okay then. No one is forcing anyone. If you don't want to say, don't say. If you don't want to listen, don't listen," says the man drinking tea, every so often closing his eyes as though recalling something or falling asleep instantaneously, and through closed eyelids he sees, almost fondles, the sinewy, well-shaped legs of the woman drinking coffee, the woman whose profile reminds him of his mother and whose face reminds him of some woman he was passionately in love with whom he's been trying to get out of his mind for years now, though every so often getting confused, as he feels that the face of the woman drinking coffee reminds him of his mother and her profile of the woman he was passionately in love with whom still today he can't forget or even alleviate the weight of her memory, though again without being a hundred percent sure, given that his mother stubbornly refused to have her photo taken full face and would only be photographed in profile, which is why the only full-face photos of his mother that he recalls are those taken by his father with an antiquated camera, when his mother would smear her face and neck with natural clay, with white argil, or when she would lie down on the couch for her midday siesta, crossing her hands over her breast like a nun.* But because you have a presentiment, something you can smell coming, if you don't speed up, if you don't cut short your narration, if you don't slash your own story, her story, the story of you both, the story of neither of you, he'll turn tail, triumphantly interrupt you with a new question, not in order to understand or clarify something, but to turn you elsewhere, to disorient you, which is why you tense up and continue saying, *"And so what do you do then?" says the woman drinking coffee. "You sew up your mouth with a packing needle and thick thread and you stop up your ears with wax," says the man drinking tea. "And if you're somewhere where there is no packing needle or thick thread or wax?" says the woman drinking coffee. "I was speaking metaphorically," says the man drinking tea. "I understood," says the woman drinking coffee. "So then?" says the man drinking tea. "So then, what?" says the woman drinking coffee. "Didn't you understand?" says the man drinking tea. "Understand what?" says the woman drinking coffee. "I'm just saying, what do you do?" says the man drinking tea. "When?" says the woman drinking coffee. "I'm saying," says the man drinking tea. "Yes, you're saying," says the woman drinking coffee. "I'm saying, And even if with sewn-up mouth you talk and with stopped-up ears you hear?" says the man drinking tea. "Listen, then," says the woman drinking coffee. "I'm listening," says the man drinking tea. "We're cut off in a seaside hotel at the edge of the world," says the woman drinking coffee. "We, who's we?" says the man drinking tea. "So this abandoned hotel is bathed in the same ashen light day and night, summer and winter, the sea is as still as in a photograph, and the sky so heavy that sometimes you think that if you don't stoop you'll bang* your head," says the woman drinking coffee. "Nice hotel," says the man drinking tea. "You only come here to tell stories," says the woman drinking coffee. "Fine mess," says the man drinking tea. "You don't come for a vacation, you don't come for a conference," says the woman drinking coffee. "Ideal spot," says the man drinking tea. "You're no writer to turn the stories into a book, or a parent to narrate them to your children, or a politician to tout them to your voters," says the woman drinking coffee. "Paradise," says the man drinking tea. "Nor even some nutjob to bawl them at passersby," says the woman drinking coffee. "So what are you?" says the man drinking tea. "You're a wretched soul," says the woman drinking coffee. "Wretched and a soul?" says the man drinking tea. "You're a nothing, and the only thing you have, the only thing left to you, is to tell stories," says the woman drinking coffee. "Stories, what stories?" says the man drinking tea. "Stories with a beginning, middle, and end. Truncated stories. Secondhand stories. Humdrum stories. Crazy stories," says the woman drinking coffee. "Crazy?" says the man drinking tea. "Breathless stories. Stories buried alive. Stories with villains and saints," says the woman drinking coffee. "And all day long we'll tell stories?" says the man drinking tea. "And all night long. When we're eating and even when we're sleeping," says the woman drinking coffee. "You're having me on," says the man drinking tea. "Not at all," says the woman drinking coffee. "And will we manage it?" says the man drinking tea. "Everything's arranged," says the woman drinking coffee. "Arranged?" says the man drinking tea. "We'll eat and we'll tell stories. We'll sleep in shifts or we'll just doze," says the woman drinking coffee. "And what will they do with so many stories?" says the man drinking tea. "What will they do with them?" says the woman drinking coffee, though it could be tea. "Yes.

What can you do with so many different, tedious, or useless stories? When here right now, even an interesting story is being lost. Everyone has his own say here right now," says the man drinking tea, though it could be coffee. "A murky, ground, odorless stuff," says the woman drinking coffee, though it could be tea. "What? What's that?" says the man drinking tea, though it could be coffee. "That? That's what fashions them," says the woman drinking coffee, though it could be tea. "I understood that. What I haven't understood is what's that murky how did you call it?" says the man drinking tea, though it could be coffee. "The less you understand and the more stories you tell, the better for you," says the woman drinking coffee, though it could be tea. "Sometimes I think that you're playing with me and at others that you're trying to scare me," says the man drinking tea, though it could be coffee. "Bacteria, fungi, earthworms," says the woman drinking coffee, though it could be tea. "Now what are you doing?" says the man drinking tea, though it could be coffee. "Compost, topsoil, how else can I put it?" says the woman drinking coffee, though it could be tea. "I see," says the man drinking tea, though it could be coffee. "What you say, what I say, what we say between us is intended for food, food for the Lumbricus rubellus," says the woman drinking coffee, though it could be tea. "I see," says the man drinking tea, though it could be coffee. "Let it go," says the woman drinking coffee, though it could be tea. "So what will happen, then, if we stop telling stories?" says the man drinking tea, though it could be coffee. "You don't want to know," says the woman drinking coffee, though it could be tea. "Just a minute, so why don't we take off?" says the man drinking tea, though it could be coffee. "You don't want to know that either," says the woman drinking coffee, though it could be tea. "And since it's so lousy here, the worms eat our stories, we can't sleep or eat, why do we bother coming?" says the man drinking tea, though it could be coffee. "Even if they put you wise to it, play dumb," says the woman drinking coffee, though it could be tea. "What have you gotten me into?" says the man drinking tea, though it could be coffee. "Even if you remember, forget it," says the woman drinking coffee, though it could be tea. "And what's the name of this crap hotel?" says the man drinking tea, though it could be coffee. "Everyone calls it what he wants," says the woman drinking coffee, though it could be tea. "And how do you say, I'm there, or I'm going there, how the hell do you do that?" says the man drinking tea, though it could be coffee. "You say I'm going somewhere else," says the woman drinking coffee, though it could be tea. "And do they understand?" says the man drinking tea, though it could be coffee. "All of them. As soon as you say, I'm going somewhere else, they catch on straightaway," says the woman drinking coffee, though it could be tea. "You've got me caught up again in more bullshit about the end of the world. For fuck's sake!" says the man drinking tea, though it could be coffee. And this man who could be drinking tea, coffee, orange juice or grapefruit juice, whiskey, rum, gin, vodka, tequila, or simply water, because you don't know, asks you, *If at this very moment you weren't here, if you weren't answering my questions, where would you want to be, and what would you want to be doing?* When you hear that question, a question indicative of his mood, and so of your question-and-answer relationship, formulated exactly in this way or perhaps with a slight variation, you know deep inside that the moment has arrived for the mouse, the cement, the cloud, the granite, the marble, the ash, the coal. The moment of the Gray Studio has arrived. Walls, carpets, lighting, pictures. Dark gray, light gray, gray gray and silvery gray, bluish gray, warm gray. It goes without saying that everyone inside, sound engineers, secretaries, cleaners, couriers, all wear gray. The men gray suits or gray overalls, the women gray two-piece outfits, gray overalls. Perhaps that's why you don't encounter any plants at all inside there. Even the light inside the Gray Studio is dense, heavy, resembling an overcast sky. So the moment you hear, *If at this very moment you weren't here,* you know that something is changing, something is beginning not to be as it was before. First of all, you cease to be what you think you are. A simple interviewee, informally being analyzed, gently being interrogated, or however else you define yourself. From that moment on you are called *Female Connection 7591.* Whereas he, the one who voiced the question, that decisive question, the one who asks, the one who only ever asks, the one who will always ask, is called *Administrator.* And all this is not just hanging in the air. It's consolidated and certified. Between you there is a cooperation protocol, a *memory work contract* signed by you as *Connection* and him as *Administrator* in which the rights and obligations of both parties are set out in detail. Inside the Gray Studio your life, the life of any variable Connection, is precisely set out on a scale of pleasure or displeasure on the part of the invariable Administrator. Some women go one step farther. They feel him to be eternal. They feel him, consider him, see him. At any rate. Yet a scale which, however much it quantifies the degree of attraction, indifference, or repulsion on the part of the Administrator to your answers, always leaves a margin for readjustment of the fixed gradations. The only invariable, nonnegotiable and invariable point, explicitly specified between you, is that your answers, the answers of all the Connections, from the moment that they leave your lips and spread out through the highly sensitive microphones and cables in order to be stored in completely secure digital files, no longer belong to you. In short, you are what doesn't belong to you. Yet even your inability to answer, your possible irresolution, or even your very silence do not belong to you. Since your silence is not a random or general silence. It is a silence in the face of specific questions. It is a silence that aims to deaden, to gag, to bury the questions by the Administrator. To plunge them into total oblivion. At the very best. Because beside him the unanswered questions, whether you have anything to say or not, whether you refuse to answer, even if you consider it all the same to answer or not to answer, exude something disagreeable. They don't smell so pleasant. Burnt rubber, stale fish, toxic waste. They're unbearable. You can't bear them. They have something of an unburied corpse, of despoiled remains. Since the only thing that belongs to you here is the inalienable right of the Administrator to expel you, to dispel you, to displace you, to throw you out of the Gray Studio. Forever or temporarily. It's then that you fall, correspondingly, into the category of the *Unconnected* or *Former Connections*. Though not without warning. Everything here is mild, graded. No spasmodic act. Foreshadowed. No surprise. You have previously been warned and warned again. The blue, green, yellow, and red lights have all flashed many times in front of the comfortable, soft armchair in which you're sitting—it's said that it's made of fine alligator skin. The colored escalations every day, every hour, every minute reflect your *narrative curve*, and consequently your *communication chart*. Therefore, the ordeals that follow, the foreseen ordeals, those that you cosigned in the *memory work contract*, if nothing else, do not surprise the Connected with a nonexistent *narrative curve* and zero *communication chart*. Insomnia, artificial panic fits, migraine bouts, allergic shocks, as well as mild electric discharges and short cold showers are part of the *awareness menu*. No, the Gray Studio is not a place for torture, elimination, or correction. Here the only thing tested, the only thing scanned, the only thing recorded is the length of response of those Connected. Their participating nucleus. The centripetal and centrifugal propensities of that outer layer of desire. Since it's well known that your answers are not only answers, whether convincing or not, delightful or not, but above all are indexes that create an oscillograph of the range of your very existence, of your course, of your presence in the Gray Studio. Though sometimes you feel, not knowing whether other Connections, those Disconnected, or Former Connections have similarly felt, that the Gray Studio exists and doesn't exist. Given that you receive questions like those posed here by the Administrator as SMS messages on your cell phone, or as e-mail messages in your inbox. Even as notes that you find in the most unthinkable places in your home or your office. And also in coded routes, at the most unexpected times, in the most improbable spots, routes that you're called upon to decode and locate. It's then that you feel that the Gray Studio, apart from a Gray Studio, is something more worrying, more vague, something borderline. It's then that you feel that the tangible Gray Studio, with its unspeaking, unruffled workers and its rigid rules, resembles a mound of candy, a cartoon nightmare, compared to the immaterial, diffuse Gray Studio, that terrifying ubiquitous gray of absence. But no, this time you're not going to do him the favor. No. You're not going to become once again, for the umpteenth time, his source of alleviation. A hundred times no. Let him take a turn, smash everything, relegate you to those Disconnected. He won't hear again of legends and traditions about the Gray Studio from your lips. Curtain fall.

So instead of the dystopian fairy tale that relieves him, affirms him, elevates him, replying to that *if you weren't here* and all the rest, you say to him, *I might be climbing a railed wooden staircase wearing a mustard-colored silk blouse, a thin pleated woolen skirt, and flat brown shoes, after just having seen on TV an adolescent, a fair-skinned boy no more than fifteen years old, his head shaved, though it could also be a dark-skinned girl with Rasta hair, under twenty, entering their school with automatic guns and killing eight of their schoolmates, two teachers, the principal's dog, which lunged at them, before shooting themselves in the head, though I could also be descending the steps of the Metro wearing an olive-green raincoat, black suede boots, having coated my lips with deep mauve lipstick, at the moment that three deafening explosions fill the air with dust, black smoke, screams, sirens, while running round about me are squads of heavily armed police and special army units, yet there's also a strong probability that I'm sitting absentmindedly, wearing a white T-shirt, a pink linen skirt, and black espadrilles, leaning over a cup of iced vanilla tea and a half-eaten croissant at an airport where for some time successive announcements have been foretelling, warning of a tsunami, though without also excluding the possibility that I'm holding a yellow umbrella with black spots, wearing gray galoshes and a black oilskin while attempting to cross a flooded road in a chaotic metropolis, following prolonged and torrential rainfall, or even that I'm traveling by train, in the opposite direction to which it's going, wearing jeans and sandals, with my hair wrapped in a tiled scarf with geometric patterns and myself absorbed in a thick detective novel, when, from the front coaches are heard cries, screams, English mixed with Russian and Arabic, the sound of people fighting, of things being broken, or, in the final analysis, that I'm in bed burning up with fever, dozing, when, in the dead of night, my cell phone rings, so I answer and hear my first love from my schooldays, my childhood love dismembered, some years earlier, in a terrorist attack on a synagogue, though he might also have been drowned in a rubber dinghy with refugees or struck by lightning in an open space, and yet I hear his voice as clearly as a bell, as clearly as if he were standing right beside me, at my pillow, applying cool compresses to my forehead or rubbing my back with liniment, this my first and last great love.* Succinctly and explicitly, you say to him that you would want to be anywhere else than the Gray Studio. However disagreeable, ugly, or dangerous it may be. Just as long as you're not in the Gray Studio you could be any other woman apart from a Connection. End. Since Administrator without Gray Studio and Connections doesn't exist, is inconceivable. And you'll persist in not referring at all to the Gray Studio. Even if you know that by simply talking again and again about the realm of gray you'll escape from the realm of gray. Since the more you mention the Gray Studio—not necessarily positively or ecstatically, you might also bring it back into the discussion negatively or grotesquely, involve it indirectly, just so long as you don't ignore it completely, keep it hushed up, but give space to it, psychological, narrative, dreamlike space—the more you increase, multiply the possibilities that at some moment he will ask, ask you, *What's your opinion of me? You can speak openly and frankly.* A question, de facto, that he asks one in a thousand women. Some of them plan or machinate for years. To the degree that they can plan or engage in machinations with someone like himself. As a rule, however, they fear it, are afraid of it, repulse it. Of course, there are women, there always are, who fantasize about it, who are always trying it on in the mirror. Yet in the end, the ones who have answered in reality can be counted on the fingers of one hand. Anyway it's a fact that once he's asked you to size him up, to share your taste for him, even to take a position with regard to him, you've passed into the last level. Though it could be the one after the last. You're now counted, included, belong among the *Post-Connections*. A final and irrevocable upgrading. Given that a Post-Connection enjoys and has privileges that the Connections can't even begin to imagine. In other words, apart from the fact that they have the right to bypass a certain number of questions, without any obvious reason, simply because they have nothing to say, or they're feeling down, are irritated by the questions or left totally indifferent, they also have the rare privilege, the unique opportunity, of asking the Administrator three questions. In other words, the world turned on its head. And from being condemned to the wilderness of the questionee, they arrive at the oasis of the questioner. Of course, whether being a questioner with him is an oasis is open to investigation. At any rate, they are justified in expecting, and even more, deserve clarity and transparency from their former questioner. And in keeping with their judgment or their humor they can even interrupt him or mislead him through cunning or intricate questions. And in this way not only becoming Connected Administrators, Administrators in the place of the Administrator, albeit temporarily, and also, why not, igniting within him the spark of an answer, the flame of dialogue, the warmth of give-and-take. Anyhow, if he were to put that question to you, you would neither jump down his throat nor curse him to high heaven, nor would you lose your tongue, nor however would you strive to bring him onto the path of interlocution, to awaken within him the enjoyment or the peace of verbal cohabitation, as is done, as you've heard is done, by most of the female Post-Connections. Though this piece of information most probably, no not most probably, you're certain, is concocted, carefully planned, and, given that he wants to pull the strings, spread about by him. Because, as you make him out, and you can get a good idea about someone from his voice and questions, he puts this question to women who are mindless, vacant, spineless, who no longer have the curiosity, the strength, or even the energy to look at themselves in the mirror, never mind ask him something or, even less, to put themselves in a position of confrontation with him. Which is why the stage of Post-Connection within you translates into postponement, cancellation, mutilation. It smells of formalin. How else can you put it? Which is why you start to answer his questions meaningfully, not half-heartedly, offended, or distracted, going the whole hog, once the question, the curiosity, the excitement concerning who in the end was doing the asking had abated, had calmed inside you. Is it an out-of-body experience? Is it the self playing games? Is it a severe breakdown of the subject? Or perhaps, passing over to the other side, momentarily putting yourself in his position, you feel that you are dealing with a manic collector of voices and that you are nothing but one of the thousands of cases that he records? With an artist desperately trying to feed his lost inspiration? With an embittered lover who visits you in your sleep, during your fever, when you're at your worst, in order to torment you? With a brilliant, retiring researcher who has chosen you as a guinea pig for his dubious schemes? You don't know. Perhaps "I answer" equals "I exist"? If, however, he asked you, and you weren't, it goes without saying, one step away from formalin, you'd say to him, *First hypothesis, that we both exist. We continue to talk, to be silent, to exchange verbal and mental baggage till we become*

astral dust, peat, manure, fertilizer, zero. Second hypothesis, that
one of us exists. First possibility: the one who is in existence con-
tinues to ask and answer, like the solitary chess player devising clever
defenses and even cleverer offensives with his imaginary opponent.
Second possibility: eventually the one who exists grows tired of
bouncing back off the void, sinks into depression or becomes deliri-
ous. Third hypothesis, that neither of them exists. We are an imma-
terial dyad that might by chance have to face the unforeseen or even
be condemned to the most impervious extroversion, to believing that
we exist. Is there another hypothesis? Always. Our situation may not
be stable and definite. So that strange combinations may be created.
On odd-numbered days the first hypothesis may hold true, on even-
numbered days the second with its two possibilities, and on Sundays
and holidays the third hypothesis. Then probably, because he feels
you somewhat distracted or distant, though he gives no obvious in-
dication of this, to the degree that you are answering quite readily
and with sufficient clarity, he asks you, *Do you consider that you are*
prone to accidents or not? Without giving it much thought you say,
I'd put it the other way round: Are accidents prone to me? I can do
myself an injury with anything. All I need is a piece of paper to cut
myself deeply. While all around me the air is continually coming up
with obstacles. Steps and potholes, ditches appear out of nowhere,
wardrobes, boulders, tables, stakes, chairs, or cracks sprout up from
anywhere. Without my getting on to internal accidents. Sprains,
breaks, burns. What doesn't show. Things that don't heal. On the
other hand, I think that the frequency and the ease with which I
break my arm, dislocate my shoulder, bang my knee, bump my head
are not connected so much with the fact that I'm constantly else-
where, my mind is always somewhere else, I live with ten other

women, but with the blind belief that I have in my body. That's what happens when you do ballet from childhood and then you leave it. Calamities from excessive flexibility, have you heard of that? And instead of him saying something, a word, of him coming out at least with some sound recalling a roar, a whistle, a grunt, a bleat, a croak, he says, *In your life, in your daily routine, do you see the glass half-full or half-empty?* And with the momentum of the previous question, almost without breathing or batting an eye, you say to him, *I'd like to state in advance that there's often a hysteron proteron to the half-full or the half-empty glass, since more importantly there's the question of the glass itself, of the glass qua glass. Does it exist or doesn't it exist? Do we see it or are we imagining it? Nevertheless if we solve this prerequisite or if we bypass it, I can say that sometimes they call me Cortisol (Corti to my close friends) and sometimes Oxytocin. This just as a general fact. If I were to paint it, I'd say that sometimes I wear gray, dark, or earthy colors, the usual ones for a Cortisol, and at others light colors, pastel or ocher, those that suit an Oxytocin. But if I'm to be honest, precise, and to remain with my feet on the ground, I ought to say, to admit, to state that normally I sleep (in the way I sleep), wake (in the way I wake), eat (in the way I eat), speak (in the way I speak), work (in the way I work), think (in the way I think), walk (in the way I walk), cry (in the way I cry), and get angry (in the way I get angry) like a true Cortisol. Only exceptionally do I sleep, wake, eat, speak, work, think, walk, cry, and get angry like an Oxytocin.* When, once again, he interrupts you, bringing you down to earth in order to ask you, *Lady Cortisol and more rarely Lady Oxytocin, what kind of relationship do you have with money? Are you open-handed or tight-fisted?* And, in fact, what happens when you don't answer what they ask you? Without our groping to find the deeper reason. You don't answer. Maybe the question is repeated. Perhaps more forcibly. There's the possibility that the one asking might get annoyed and never ask you again. Nothing. Absolutely nothing. Though it's not improbable that he'll go on to the next question and come back to it again later. Or for it to atrophy, fade, be forgotten. Of course, these questions, and others that might arise, have to do with a normal conversation, a standard interview, a regulated conference, a fixed interrogation, a particular experiment. No answer is an answer. A good motto. I can't deny. Concise. Voluminous. Dynamic. But here, no answer means, Woe betide you. No answer leads to side effects. Obesity, hair growth, osteoporosis, spasms, disorientation, insomnia, anxiety, nerves, depression. Do you want more? Hypertension, parchedness and frequent urination, nausea, vomiting, slow healing of wounds, increased optical pressure. You come out with them all jumbled up. As they come to you. Hyper-perspiration, telangiectasis and dermatological distortions, the more characteristic being violet streaks. And selenomorphic mug. That's really something. You swell up like the inner tube of a tire. Which is why, without wasting time, you say to him, *The way you said it like that, my mind went elsewhere. Anyhow. I have no faith at all in those who say, maintain, proclaim that they're not interested in money. This for starters. On the other hand, I feel oppressed by the money machines who live only to make money, to put it in the bank and gloat over it. Second. The only ones I understand are the pathological skinflints, the ones hooked on hoarding. You can see them, how they suffer, pine, hurt when they have to spend. They squeeze themselves. And squeeze again. So those who regard money as excrement aren't far wrong. I go through phases. Sometimes I live like an ant, at others like a grasshopper. I just don't* shout it from the rooftops. There are periods when I don't throw away as much as a crumb, and periods when I throw away whole loaves. And I haven't seen shit in my sleep. Ever. Nor have I ever won the lottery, or inherited anything. Nothing. Ever. And though you might go on listing the side effects of the possibly improper responsive behavior, such as an increase in androgens, amenorrhea, and reduced libido, at the same time you wonder, wonder about something extremely ambitious, is it possible, if it's possible, for you not to answer and for you not to be transformed into an insufferable Lady Cortisol? It's precisely at that moment that he asks you, *Are you at all concerned by your origins? Do you think that you are still living in the shadow of your parents or have you freed yourself from their presence?* You answer as though you were listening to your voice on a tape recorder, sometimes slowed down and sometimes speeded up. You say to him, *Was my father a just man, spineless, or a depressive? Was my mother an attractive woman, did she have lovers, or was she an alcoholic? Did my brother and sister stand by me, did they exploit me beyond measure, or were they more strangers to me than strangers? Was my grandma a wonderful cook, did she tell cannibalistic fairy tales or fart shamelessly? Did my uncle adore travel, was he an amazing mimic, or did he secretly grope me? Was my cousin a math genius, did he tell lame jokes, or was he a malicious asshole? Was my female cousin a talented pianist, did she laugh madly, or did she systematically hit on all my boyfriends? And so forth. In short, I can't stand the family historical digging. All that dust, all that imperative, pressing suffering, all that butchering of recollections, all that memory tribunal. I can't stand that merry-go-round of what kind of family do you hail from? No. You tear up nothing. Neither prettifying, nor cannibalizing. We don't touch on our roots. We*

neither uproot them nor water them. We leave them in peace. To be
forgotten. So they'll forget us and we them. In any case, whether we
eat our insides out or shake the dust from our feet, we're chasing our
own tail. At the same time, you wonder how long that forbearing
though weary muscle, that dark muscle, which some call death of
the visible, others exquisite melodies, others a den of beasts, others
scorched earth, but most call the heart, will be able to go on supporting our real, though mainly our imaginary, weight. In other
words, if—and interrupting your silent train of thought he asks you,
Are you afraid of death? Do you think about it? Is it something that
worries you, does it affect your daily life or do you live as if it didn't
exist? Ignoring first of all the fact that he is interrupting you ever
more often, second how the particular question connects with the
previous answer, and third what the fuck he has in his head and in
his heart, you say to him, *When I hear that question, I immediately*
think of another question, a question that they don't put to me, nor
does it arise, at least not directly, head-on, from that question about
death, but one that is stimulated inside me, awakened, when they
ask me if I'm afraid of death, if I think about it, if it's something that
worries me, if it affects my daily life or if I live as if it didn't exist, in-
side me I hear, and no I'm not hard of hearing nor do I hear voices,
the question "Do you usually arrive early, or late, or are you on time
for your appointments?" So my answer, de facto, will attempt, will
have as its aim to satisfy the self-supplying indirect question, without
of course my underestimating the gravity or the importance of the
more obvious question. So before I give my time reference, I'd like to
clarify some suppressed aspects of the meeting. First of all, what kind
of meeting are we talking about? Romantic, professional, social,
friendly, family, dreamy, or metaphysical? First thing to bear in

mind. Is it a meeting that I'm longing to go to, that I can't wait for, is my heart beating madly, are my limbs numb, am I paralyzed, or one that I don't even want to think about, that I shy away from, or am I totally indifferent, neither hot nor cold? This too has its role to play. Also the duration. Is it insignificant? It's one thing to know that the meeting will last half an hour or an hour, and another thing not to know what's going to happen. Will you extricate yourself in a day, a week, a month, a year? More? Never? Whether it's for your own good, or not. Also, very important, is the one you're going to meet someone you know, someone familiar, or a stranger; someone you think of persistently, someone you desire, or someone you've encountered in a dream? At the same time, perhaps you're afraid of the person you're going to meet because you've heard or you have a presentiment that he's charming, a behind-the-scenes type, manipulative, someone who is constantly changing. But I don't want to make you dizzy with all my talk. I'm not saying all this in order to pretend to be clever, complex, or sour. I just believe that the internal clock, that which sometimes unwinds and deregulates the external one, changes, undermines, shakes the question's center of gravity, its ballast, from a precise time or violation to the main person in the meeting, to the motives and the aim of every meeting, in other words from something general, commonly accepted, and unquestionable to something individual, personally verifiable, and open to misinterpretation, given that sometimes time is time, but this doesn't prevent it at other times from promoting itself or at others from defaming itself, in other words—and going for a straight run of interruptions, he asks you, Do you often have recourse to lies? Or do you always try to tell the truth? Whatever you say, it'll be a lie, you think to yourself. Besides, aren't there lies that burn with the flame of truth and truths that are lies in disguise? Which is why you answer, *If you tell lies, you suffer.* *If you tell the truth, you suffer—but at least you tell the truth. If you don't say anything, you suffer.* Do you suffer because you don't know what's true and what's a lie? Do you suffer because you know that whether you tell the truth or a lie you're going to suffer? Or do you suffer because fewer and fewer people have the need to hear your truths or your lies? The unquestionable point is that you suffer. Your constant. Your root base. You're terrified when you think of what might happen if you cease to suffer. Eventually. If the narcosis reaches down to the bone. Eventually. If the anesthetization heralds a new age of suffering. Of insensible suffering. Eventually. Suffering that will require more and more suffering in order to suffer. And you'll eventually suppress that "eventually" in "never." It won't escape you. And though you want to stretch your legs, you don't even think of getting up or stretching, as you're unaware of whether you're sitting or lying down, or rather you know, but it's of no importance whether you're sitting, lying, walking, or running from the moment you answer his questions, and he asks you, *Are you in the habit of returning to old stories?* After reflecting that, at bottom, we are those who loved us, tormented us, forgave us, neglected us, or cared for us. And therefore their stories. The ones they told us, half-told us, or concealed from us. Which is why, stealing from all their lips, cracked ones, wet ones, pursed ones, open ones, sealed ones, stories with beginning, middle, and end, only with a tail, headless ones or with hacked bodies, stories that pretend to be stories, flattened stories, buried beneath other stories, stories with heart in mouth, stories like funeral gifts, you say to him, *She was hard of hearing, which is why her ears detached themselves from her head, became butterflies, black ones with yellow spots, and flew far off to* bring her the most silent melodies, songs that still haven't [. . .] he scratched his nose that sprouted high on his forehead and descended humplike down to his nonexistent lips, separating two washy, two painfully washy blue eyes, which is why [. . .] struggling in the depth of his dark eyes, like wrestlers caked in oil, were lust and mysticism, at the same moment that [. . .] her mouth was a small shriveled hole full of shrieks and grievances, which is why [. . .] when you go I don't want to wash your glass, to rub my cheek with your touch, to air my bedroom with your presence. Does it sound childish or funny? Maybe. I feel that I want to freeze time, to stupefy the moment, which, as might be expected, can neither be frozen nor stupefied, to keep, to bring back the moment, which can neither be kept nor brought back, when you drank from my glass, you put your hand on my cheek, you filled my room with the bitter smell of your existence, which is why [. . .] we gazed at each other, knowing that there was always someone else observing us. Staring at us. Scrutinizing us. This someone else, this stranger, this other was what we said and what we didn't say. So this man, then, [. . .] wore a suit that was black like the darkness, boots the color of blackberries, and he was white like death. Standing beside him was she. Motionless. Beneath the hot purple eye of the sun. Her face was like a washed rooftile. Her wide hips recalled a wooden trough. When she got up, he [. . .] thought, No, I'm not convinced by those who say they believe in nothing. They're lying. They are liars. Our passions prove that there is both eternity and zero. They prove it glaringly. It's then that I fear madness more than death. Which is why I became impassive, distant. Cold. She, all the while that he was opening his heart to her, [. . .] had a calm look, and whenever she was about to say something, her voice faded, abated with her every phrase, as though the air

around her had run out. And so [. . .] she gazed at you, without say-
ing anything, gazed at you protractedly, not only with her intensely
brown slit eyes but also with her puffy cheeks and her tight breasts
and her long, white neck. And that persistent look, from the waist up,
engulfed you, you felt it, it engrossed you like a psalm, like a rus-
tling, like a sweet nothing, as though you were [. . .] close to the bor-
der, on the edge, at the quivering, where you remember everything at
least more or less, where [. . .] between outrageous clarity and out-
rageous obscurity my life unfolded. A little clarity, a little obscurity,
a little chiaroscuro. The sweet chaos of existence. And of course, [. . .]
"Life ends, if it ends, when you get tired, when you're constantly
glum, can't be bothered to wake up, take unpleasant dreams at face
value, extend them into your daily life, try to correct them, to ap-
pease them, till eventually you refuse to get out of bed, you con-
stantly pretend to be ill so they'll take care of you, all the familiar
stuff, that is," he said, and added, [. . .] "I'd gladly drink another ab-
sinthe to her health, but I've forgotten whether she's dead or whether
I've lost touch with her, because we've drifted apart, haven't spoken
for over ten years," he said, and [. . .] then she reflected intensely, as
though replying to him, though she didn't reply, didn't even look at
him, or rather she looked at him with her neck bent like a lily, and
with her breathless thought she said to him, "The moment you look
at me, all the zippers, inside and outside, all the linings, the stitches,
all the skin's hidden cracks vanish, my skin becomes skin again, in
other words that naked, unmediated, primeval loneliness. Of course
I'm not going to let you come near me, that's never going to happen
between us" [. . .], and she remained motionless, perspiring, in a bes-
tial position, sinking into the snow-white mire of the sheets. And like
a relay race, perhaps seeking to have the previous question pene-

trate into the following, to merge the one into the other, he asks you, *What's the most powerful, the most indelible erotic scene that has engraved itself in your memory?* Before you can determine whether the question leaves you a sweet, bitter, salty, greasy, tart, sour, or neutral taste, you've already answered. *Then it's almost daybreak. Then he falls silent. Then he says to me, "I want to sleep on your disgusting slit." Then he looks at me as though he were looking at a forest at night. Then he falls asleep. Then he murmurs something in his sleep. Then he clasps me strongly round my neck. Then I jerk my legs. Then he wraps me in black canvas and ties me tightly with thick yellow cord. Then he drags me like a sack and pushes me into the trunk of his car. Then we arrive at a lake. Then he opens the trunk but I'm not there. Then he screams without being heard. Then he returns home. Then it's almost daybreak again. Then daybreak doesn't come.* And as though the snout of the previous question had got a sniff of the groin of the next one, he says to you, *And, to have a good question, how do you imagine your final moments?* Feeling as though you were asking yourself, as though you were listening to the echo of a silent thought, seeing the undulation of a faded image, you say to him, *Surrounded by my nearest and dearest in a quiet house encircled by a well-tended garden; discarded on a trundle bed in a wretched hospital, shitting myself out of fear of* this is where it ends; *flung face down in a ditch, raped and knifed in the chest and neck; sweaty and exhausted amid a cluster of uninhibited phalli, arms, and thighs, a final, farewell orgy with forgotten, dumped, or dead lovers; weeping and screaming, mixing saliva, mucus, and cries while leaving this fucking here below for the even more fucking up above; eating my favorite coffeecake and getting stuck into it forever; laughing constantly, uncontrollably, till I become a woman who*

laughs her heart out and expires with terrible chest spasms, with pro-
longed stomach cramps, of unbearable pains in her dislocated jaw;
dancing and singing till my heart bursts songs by Chuck Berry, Bert
Berns, and by Björk and Winehouse; remaining silent for days with
eyes closed and lying on the bed, not eating anything, not drinking
anything, without any need to defecate or urinate, till all those
around me confirm that I'm not only convincingly imitating the art
of the deceased, but that I have become what I'm imitating, which is
why they'll make haste to speak with a funeral parlor for all the rest;
thinking about only the deepest kisses, the most secret caresses that
I gave in my life, the most beautiful songs that I heard, the strangest
dances that I danced, the most indescribable places that I saw; sleep-
ing and waking suddenly, seeing my parents by my bed, young and
in love, before they gave birth to me, before they were married, before
they became implacable enemies, my father wearing a white linen
suit and barefoot, my mother wearing a sugar-colored dress, high-
heeled sandals, with her hair wet, it's dusk, though it could also be
dawn, in the distance can be heard persistent twittering and muted
barking, I want to tell them that my belly is hurting so they'll notice
me, give me a little attention, but I hesitate because I wonder how
they can concern themselves with me when I still don't exist, when
they still haven't brought me into the world? At the same time I don't
want to interrupt their passionate gazes with my miserable con-
cocted tummy-ache, seeing them like that self-contained and im-
mersed in desire, each swooning at the sight of the other, and I reflect
that they may not even get round to the business of procreation, their
passion might be consumed as passion and so their resulting fruit
might not have to experience the theater of cruelty and its even
crueler backstage scenes; at the moment that it's accomplished, will

I dream of my present, listen to sweet melodies, smell fragrant pas-
tures and other such bullshit, or will I be as white as chalk from the
darkness about to fall upon me? And after he first involves you in
conversations, images, and thoughts that have the rattle of death, he
then takes you in another direction, *And if they were to ask you,* he
asks, *to think of a title for all that's happening here, what would it*
be? Title? you repeat, trying to assess how he sees you, how he re-
gards you. As material for a newspaper or magazine article? As a
sound installation at an art exhibition? As documentation at an aca-
demic conference? As a means of filling his own void? Nevertheless, you come out with a list of titles. "Interview with a Dead
Woman," "Someone to Hurt Them," "What Things Fall," "Stories
with No Story," "Final Matters," "Nobody's Room," "Theory of
Tiredness," "Burnt Violet." And letting out a sound, something between a yawn and blowing one's nose, or rather a yawn reinforced
by blowing one's nose, though possibly also a yawn that occasioned
blowing one's nose, rather than the opposite, he asks you, *Generally*
speaking, do you consider yourself to be likable or dislikable? You
want to open up the topic. To get some things clear right from the
start. For example, you want to say that it depends always on who
likes you and who dislikes you. But also whether you and the one
who likes or dislikes you have the same or a corresponding hierarchy
of elation or dejection over a whole list of things. Since like or dis-
like at first sight rarely happens, and when it does happen it has the
air of desire. This and much more goes through your mind before
you say to him, *I'd say that I have neither any real friends nor any*
real enemies. At the smallest hardship the former leave me, the latter
disappear at my first, mild reaction. As though they didn't exist, as
though they existed solely as obsessions. There are times when I think

that I'll die without friends and enemies. And because it's easier to become dislikable or hated, I aim to acquire enemies, lots of enemies. Before I get old. Lots and lots. As long as my legs still carry me. Since they're not going to remember me for my humor, my kindness, or my good manners, at least let them remember me for my morbid and withdrawn character. Not to mention that, years later, they may even forgive you for the wrong you did them. Though better that they re-call you as forever detestable. A thousand times better. What? Drown in respectable disregard and honest oblivion? No, I don't understand that. More likely, you don't understand. So, enemies! Urgently. Do I have time, what do you think? As if he'd answer you. Just harps on to his own tune. A regular jackass. And with a connected question, in a similar vein, he continues, *So do you think that you're pleasant or unpleasant company?* He's a jackass, but you're one too. *I don't know. Honestly. On the other hand, I wonder, do people keep company today? I usually pass by unnoticed. Once they told me that I was, that I functioned, as a pacifier. I became the catalyst in tense circumstances. Satiated friendships, broken relationships, couples in crisis. That once is now long dead. Probably. Now I'm beyond un-pleasantness and enjoyment. But lately something has taken hold of me. For no reason I suddenly want to be provocative. To throw fat in the fire. Rub salt in the wounds. Be divisive. But again I have the antidote. I think to myself that becoming unpleasant doesn't auto-matically mean that you become something special. All around you there are so many unpleasantly unpleasant people. That's what I think of when I become hell bent on being the most unpleasant woman in the world. Not at all easy. So that not even your breath can stand you. No one. Not even Unpleasantness. So that even this, on seeing you, will take to its heels. And then it's as if my fever falls.*

I become empty. I bid farewell to the bad energy. I become empty. The neglected little girl once again gets her breath back. Inside me. I become empty. As if he'd let you empty yourself. He wants you cornered, choked up, panicked, in utter confusion. Banging on the walls of your own self. Your teeth chattering, your ears buzzing, your hands trembling, your legs buckling. But above all, he wants you to be a huge eczema so you won't approach anyone and no one will approach you. Untouchable. Unapproachable. And naturally it's the moment, the fitting moment, any more fitting is unimaginable, for him to ask you, *At this moment, at this very moment that we're speaking, what are you most in need of?* This time he'll get it pushed down his throat. You'll tell him straight. If he listens to anything other than his own icy-shitty-screwy voice. *Shut up, jerk. That's what I long to shout. Let everything stop. Let them all put a sock in it. Shut it, jerk. I don't want to hear a thing. Not even a pin drop. Yet no one is listening to me. Have I lost my voice? Has the whole universe gone deaf? Which is why I prefer not to have to decide about anything. Never again. Not to have to decide about anything. But to be practical, useful, and self-sufficient like a chair. Apathetic like a chair. Whether they dust me or polish me. Whether I'm sat on by kids, the overweight, or those covered in shit. And if they get angry and smash me to pieces? There! And if they get cold and throw me into the fireplace? There! It would have been better, though, now that I think about it again, if I'd met people who would have softened time's rough curve for me. Without saying anything. Without doing anything. Just simply because they breathe. But where am I to find them? Are there streets, squares, restaurants, bars, countryside places, crawling with people or empty, frequented by these inconspicuous types, these wonderful personalities, whose lives are not yet hell?* Not a clue. Unperturbed. Same old tune. *And if something could change in you, with one single movement, alle uno, alle due, alle tre? What would it be?* Same old tune from him, same old tune from you. *To stop putting myself in the other's shoes. Which is why I'm unable to stand on my feet anywhere. To look anyone in the eye. Because facing me I always have someone like me. But not me. Some who are sadder than me, angrier than me, more vulnerable than me. Some that I need to come close to, to listen to, to help. Putting myself aside, being less sad, which I'm not, being less angry, which I'm not, being less vulnerable, which I'm not, putting myself aside, having no one like me to come close to me, to listen to me, to help me. But eventually I'll come out of the state of no self and put myself in the place of self. Then you, not you personally, but all you with the grand, plethoric, overbearing self, will vanish. Both you and your questions too. Your notorious questionnaire will be consumed by the blackness. At last! The day will come, I know, when I'll again hear the wind, the silence, the sea. I'm certain. I'll again hear pretty melodies, thundering, revving, shouting, gunshots. Without me confusing any sound, anything at all, with your voice. That chaotic nothingness has a sellby date. Doesn't it?* And there's a sound as though of something breaking. Did a glass that he was holding fall? Was there a small explosion in his space? Did he perhaps collapse to the floor? Nothing happened. As if anything could. He returns to ask, with the most frothy cynicism, *I always wanted to ask you, how do you feel after my questions?* Right then. You'd tell him, without the slightest intention of vexing him or galling him, that sometimes you feel as though you're flicking through the pages of an endless book, a book in which stories are continually being added, in which the protagonists keep multiplying like amoebas, in which the events mirror new events and more new events, as though its pages were being split in two and three in perpetuity, at other times that you feel you can hear a meat machine mincing you, bones, fat, nerves, and flesh become a bloodied, mixed-up mass, inextricable, with direct, pregnant, original, or subversive questions, which, the more direct, pregnant, original, and subversive they are, the more velvety is your mincing, though usually, you'll make it clear to him, after some questions of his, not only those that he considers pointed, direct, original, and subversive, but also those that he considers inferior, tired, or indifferent, the only thing you can do, the only thing left to you, is to slap yourself until your mouth bleeds, eat so much chocolate and drink so much cognac that you vomit all day long, go out stark naked into the streets singing as much out of key as you can the songs that you'd connected with unpleasant, extremely unpleasant, events. This then. And if things get too intense, if they reach a limit, you get into your tub of hot water and, after first masturbating, if you can, you slash your wrists, which you certainly can. But all this he's not going to hear from you. Not from you. Let one of the other women tell him. No. No, you're not ashamed either of yourself or of him. It's the word you're ashamed of. The words. The images. Even the spaces between the words and the images. You feel so ashamed. Ashamed. Ashamed. Ashamed. That shame could drive you crazy. Which is why you'll seal your lips. Keep your mouth shut. Sew it up with the most resolute silence. With the most furious denial. Nothing. Cessation. Void. The breath of the dead. For as long as he can take it. Let him set in motion whatever he wants. Let him use psychological or physical violence. The breath of the dead. The end. But he does nothing. He can't even take it for half an hour. Because he knows you. He knows your limits. *When you were young*, he asks you, *what did you like doing most?* Is he backing off? Is he starting to back off? Time will tell. You answer him, however, as though nothing were amiss. All tiptop. All fine. *Being silent*, you say to him. *Not playing or reading or fondling myself. Just being silent. There were days, even, when I forgot to talk. I'd wrap myself in silence like little girls wrap themselves in their coats, in the arms of Mommy or Daddy, in the gaze of a boy. No one concerned themselves much with me. That's the truth. At least I escaped all the lectures. There were times when I'd dream of that silence. But one more pure, more tender, more calm. There was no shadow of spite or resignation to adulterate it.* In that slight pause between the closing of your mouth and the opening of his, you're sure that the next question will be about your sleep. You've learned something after being with him for so long. With him in a manner of speaking. His mouth in a manner of speaking. Since only rarely, very rarely, do you wonder about the face behind that voice, the eyes, ears, and nose, and how it's embodied in a chest, back, groin, limbs. Is he fair or dark-skinned? Is he lean or flabby? Very rarely, when you feel that time is passing gently between you both, in other words once in a while, almost never, you want to see something more, to touch something more, to smell something more, to kiss something more, to lick something more, to bite something more. His mouth. His dick. And, naturally, he asks you, *I'd like to know, is your sleep constant or interrupted? Do you sleep easily or with difficulty?* And while you listen to his question, you have the impression that you're listening to it from afar, but not so far for you to say that the one asking you is at the other side of town, though it might also be from close by, but not so close for you to say that the one asking you is behind you, within breathing distance, anyhow, not to spin it out too long, you have the impression that the questioner is in a spot that's neither very close nor very far away, and at any rate, wherever this fluid zone may be, this thin rind, where it's only possible to stand on your tiptoes, bells and sirens are heard coming from a distance. The tragicomic thing is that the bells are tolling ominously, as though to inform you about something bad that's happened, while the sirens are sounding out of breath and out of tune, as if some little kid were playing with his ambulance, his fire engine, or his patrol car. *Normally I sleep easily. But there are times*, you tell him, feeling that you are still standing on tiptoe, suspended, somewhere between a prancing animal and a lame ballerina, *when I fall onto the bed and don't want to wake up again. Not to wake up and find that all the things upsetting me or troubling me have changed. Not to wake up. To continue with sleep in sleep. At other times I refuse to sleep, precisely because of the fear that I won't wake up. Or that I'll wake up and won't know what exactly I was doing in my life before going to sleep. Or, worst of all, that I'll remember only a few things and jumbled, even arriving at the point of not exactly understanding the language that I spoke before going to sleep, of having unknown words, of feeling uncomfortable with those speaking to me in our common language. So there are times when I sleep like a night bird and others when I sleep like a sorrowful ghost. But often, well sometimes, to be precise, not to be precise, being precise just to be precise is not something that appeals to me, being precise because the precision inside me has significance, political, aesthetic, existential, metaphysical, magical, put it however you like; in other words, for me to be capable of what I say, what I think, and what I feel, you know what I mean, sometimes then I face sleep, not so much as a deferred state, in which, among other things, bones, muscles, and nerve tissue are re-created, but more like a chaotic workshop, like a chemical war, in which serotonin, norepinephrine, and adenosine fight with each other for where the story of the lying down with the self is finally going. On the other hand, I reflect that lying down, going to bed, means curling up with myself, limiting my existence in space, giving space to the lesser me. Then, I wonder, how does it happen that I'm interested in whether I sleep like a log or not, whether I have pleasant or unpleasant dreams, when everything around me is so defective and within me so debilitated? Or perhaps the opposite? Everything around me so debilitated and within me so defective? Or perhaps both at the same time? In other words, everything around me and inside me is debilitated and defective, and the only thing I'm looking for is a place to lie down, to park myself, to fade away, to declare myself missing, absent, inert?* For some time you've been wanting to tell him that there's no distance between the one asking and the one answering. There's no distance that has to be covered. Dialogue, conversation, addiction to questions and answers recalls, not all too rarely, the protagonist in some dark farce who falls again and again on level ground, an athlete who bursts his lungs running while fixed to the spot. But you won't tell him. Just as you won't tell him that sometimes you sit and compose something that doesn't exist. With utmost care and discipline. You spend days and nights writing down a decalogue that was never dictated to you, was never given to you, nor was it, in some indirect or inexplicable way, communicated to you. The catalogue of the female respondent. Diligent? Effective? Functional? Passive? Submissive? Let's leave it plain. Better. What's left bare is always more spacious, more inclusive. So then, how do we answer? One, straight response, without haste; two, whatever happens, we don't hold our breath; three, our breathing is so that the images and words may breathe, not us; four, we limit the tiny movements of the head and body, because they overburden, tax our voice; five, we don't come out with the words one by one, we work on the gaps between the words; six, we place the meaning between the words the way we place something familiar that's hard to find; seven, we listen to the meaning after first having exhausted, deleted all our manners, our defenses, our familiarities so as to answer as if we were saying something significant, something unique; eight, the attempt, even the hyper-attempt that we make in order to answer should pass like a breeze through what we're saying; nine, our images are more important than our image; ten, we reveal gradually, gently, as though it were self-evident, the hidden violence both of the questions and of the answers. Ten points, not so obvious. Ten footnotes, ten exhortations that you either heard or got wind of. In between his pauses. In the gaps in his thoughts. In the cracks in his voice. Possibly all this is in your head. Something between projection and longing. Because the other— can't hold true. You exclude it. That you're contriving a way to get into his position? Why are you even thinking about it? It's not possible. No way. And if you were to? In order to do what? But he who doesn't put himself in anyone else's position, not even his own, asks you, *Do you believe in God? Are there times when you call on him?* You always had a problem with the flow of his questions. There are times when you think that in front of you, you have a broken-down pinball machine. A broken chessboard. Something formerly useful, formerly entertaining. It's now clear. Hits you in the face. He confuses the lists with the questionnaires. More than clear. He's breathing his last. He's lost it. Unless what he asks is always unconnected with what he asked just previously. Whether by intention or contrivance. Unclear. Whatever the case, he's always elsewhere. And impenetrable. Concrete. And air. At the same time. You can't catch him. Anywhere. Concrete and air. That's his makeup. His raw materials. *In the past, whenever I needed him,* you say to him, *whenever I called to him, he always had something else to do. Or not do. Since, as they say, when he does nothing it's as if he were doing something. Even so. He didn't have time, he was up to the ears. Okay. And afterward he was sad. Distraught. In other words absent. That's about it. Then. Now my cheeks no longer flush from big ideas and bloated words. Enough! Besides the big ideas and bloated words sank in blood and intolerance. So? So, I couldn't give a shit. Whether he exists or doesn't exist. It's all the same to me. It doesn't concern me. How shall I put it? Personally he doesn't owe me any answer. About anything. And how could he owe me given that I don't ask him anything. I hear those who rail at him. First they curse him, then cry, then entreat him, and finally they worship him. As though he were some kind of mafia boss. All right. The boss is not always right, but he is the boss. Okay. On the other hand, do you let yourself get riled at someone who you want something from? What do you all expect from him when the only thing he knows is how not to speak? Sermons? Signs? A friendly pat on the back? That he'll help you sort yourself out? Save you from poverty, grief, or death? From what? Perhaps that he'll sweeten the passing of time? This perhaps? Soften your inside? Well. The one who is omnipresent and omnipotent does nothing for no one. By his nature. Just swallow it. Do you want to accept him as an elaborate nothing? Accept him. But only so far.* Perhaps feeling that your tone has exceeded the limits of the question, that you might involve him in your answer or outflank him, feeling weak, alone, or vulnerable, he asks you, *If I were your son and were ill or your father and were at my last, would you take care of me?* Or, like a third-rate comic, *Really, would you ever think of writing and sending me a love poem?* But also like a sentimental lackey, *What's the most extreme thing that you would dare do for me?* You hear this, and the thought comes to you. You've thought of it. And more than once. There are ways. Special gadgets that alter the voice. Allow you to be heard as you want. Specifically, a few months previously, he had become furious. *What's your relationship with your mother? Have you had or could you ever have homosexual experiences? If you had a daughter and she admitted to you that she was a lesbian, how would you react?* This doesn't bother you, of course. At all. Just the opposite. You might dig the idea that he's not a man. And that all this is a matter for women. Between you both. Strictly so. Woman to woman. A woman asks, a woman answers. With a female smell to everything. It doesn't sound too bad. Female time, female silence, female chatter. It excites you. Female juices. A lot though. Female intensity, female strategy, female indifference. Perhaps this is behind the embargo on men? Female passion. Total. He can't even stand their voices. And her hair? How is it? Short or long? Straight or wavy? And her breasts? Are they small and adolescent or full and maternal? And her slit? Is it rosy or dark? Really, how is it? Shaved, with a tattoo perhaps? Not shaggy. You rule that out. And her armpits, her neck. How does her mouth taste? Her saliva? If—it's arousing. Her heels? How are her toes? It's—it's arousing. A woman pretending to be a man. Not just dressing as a man. Not transvestitism. Besides it doesn't seem so. Not that. She wanting to hide that which—to erase the gender from her voice. To disguise it. And there's something in that. Unguarded. Yes, that. Wounded. That too. Unguarded and wounded. Yes, yes. Funnily unguarded and wounded. Funny. A funny, unguarded wound. Her mouth. A funny, irritated wound. But afterward you think about it again. You stop and think about it again. And—you're cautious. Hesitant. It can't be. Maybe you'll give something. Something of your own. You need it. You do what you need. You give her—give him. You put something over her—over him. You hang. You secure. You touch. You transfer. Otherwise—what else? Then there are other times—you feel it. You move. You change. You whirl. What else can you do? It's the only way to remain stable with him. You constantly change angles. Perspectives. Only he has a zero angle. For you, for the others like you. For himself. For everything. Only him. The chosen one. That's why you change. So as not— otherwise you can't endure. You can't endure him. And you feel that. Often. More and more often. And the more often you feel it— you don't feel it. It's, it's—something beyond what you feel. You feel what it is. He might refuse to accept that it is what you feel. Slip away. Not only from what you feel. But also from what it is. Might hide himself. Might change the topic, turn it into a joke, pull the wool over your eyes. You know him. How much risk there is in what you say. He's never going to say, *That's what I am*. As if he'd ever say it. It's done, over with. You accept it. Almost never. That's why what happens happens in the way that it happens. With him, everything is and isn't. With him? Together with him? Like driving while drunk. Not even that. Like driving without knowing how to drive. That. Specifically that. Putting the car into reverse in order to go forward, not braking at a sharp bend, fastening your seatbelt when you want to get out. And not colliding. And finally not crashing. Not because you don't crash. No, no. Not crashing simply because you don't care. Yes. You don't care if you crash. Exactly. Because inside you you've crashed again and again. Innumerable times. It's your routine. Let what is to happen happen, because what is to happen has already happened. It's your refrain. You mutter it. A little song of carefree crudity. That's what it is. Whatever is to happen la la la la la. You might even sway back and forth. Two turns of the waist, the left in front. Two turns of the waist, the right in front. That's how you feel when you answer his questions. When he asks you. With him. Only like that. Or better with them. Since you're not sure. Are you? Can you be sure with him? With him you're sure that you're never sure. That's the one thing you're sure about. How can you be sure that it's only him asking? That there's only one questioner? Are you willing to stick your neck out? Forget all that he said to you at the beginning. It was the beginning. It was still the honeymoon stage. And what kind of honey is it that you lick from a knife edge? Not to say that the beginning stinks of the end. Fish crate. A decaying carcass. State messianism. His beginning a finished beginning. So forget it. All that about uniqueness, about archetypical duality. Delete. Then the bombast brimmed over. You, him. And between you, what you wanted to ask yourself. Wanted and didn't know how. Asked without getting an answer. Or you considered anything an answer. Till he came along. And began to ask. He asked on your account. Asked in your place. Asked, asked, asked. Till you lost. The score and your place. Lost. Somehow like this the meaning became a method and the method a doctrine. And then others appeared like you. Who wanted someone to push them, to motivate them. Someone to ask them. Even if he interrupts them, even if he pressures them, even if he underestimates them. It's enough that he questions them. But the questions are often childish, boring, misleading, chaotic. And so what? It's enough that he questions them.

In any case he sees what all of you see. Women well and truly lost. Isn't that what you all are? Cast aside? Random, beleaguered, disoriented. Which is why you all turned a blind eye when others began to ask you. That's why you overlooked it. You're not stupid. Or deaf. You're dependent. Distressed. What if it's him, what if it's others like him? There's not a lot of difference. That's what you think. Because the ones who ask aren't inept. They're trained. Tough. They don't take just anyone. His vocal likenesses. Goes without saying. Faithful copies of him. With an identical form of expression as his. Tone, timbre, pauses. A voice mold. Tuned. And not only. They're ready for every eventuality. To react like him. If he interrupts you. If he leaves. If he attacks you. If he doesn't see reason as a result of the punishments. They're ready for war. Yes, some are more determined even than he is. More distant, more severe, more merciless. Some are exactly like him, and a bit more. And far beyond him. And if they're not clones of him? Because that rumor goes around. If they're relatives of his. If he has a big family? That's something that's heard too. Sons, nephews, cousins, uncles. If all that complex, labyrinthine, bureaucratic network doesn't exist? Just imagine. If we are dealing with a tight family operation. That simple. You'll say to me, Something's not right. Yes. You might imagine it and not tell me. I'll agree with you. Whatever you decide. Even if it passes like a flash through your mind. Yes. Even if in the course of things you forget it. Really. Something's not going too well. No. Not with him who's doing the asking, nor with all of us doing the answering. I'll agree. I can't. Can I not agree? Inasmuch as it concerns me. I can't. Yet there's this too. There's this. I can feel it. Don't you feel it? There's this and there's this for sure. Not always. It comes and goes. Like a tide. Like a headache. Like eczema. Like melancholy. Like a song. More rarely like a sensation. And even more rarely like consolation. It happens. Listen to me. It's not improbable. Just as you learn to eat, to defecate, to dress, to speak, to keep silent, to come, to cry, to forget, to deteriorate, that in particular, to die. Like that. Exactly like that. You also learn how to answer. No difference. You're obliged to. You learn. You answer. What they ask you. What he asks you. Him. In any case, all the questions finish with him. In any case, no one else asks you. No one else like him. There is no question without him. And when there's no question — do you want me to go on? There's not even any questionnaire. He's the first question. And the last. The question's question. And without a question. It's him. Again. No question. None. Fine. That's why. That's precisely why. You answer. Whether you like it or not. Whether you have anything to say to him or not. Whether you've settled or not on his exact identity. Finding his voice terrifying, acceptable, or indifferent. You answer. He asks. You answer. You might be in the kitchen eating or smoking, in your bathroom soaking or crying, in your office working or gazing at the clouds, you might be landing or taking off at some airport, after some business trip, a separation or a funeral. He asks, you answer. Though you might also be sleeping or waking on an endless shore, where you meet cheerful swimmers, though dead for a long time, in fact the date of their death is embroidered like a tattoo on their sunburned bodies, men, women, and children, none of whom go into the sea, no one is wet on that shore, as the sea isn't blue and has no waves, or rather the waves are still, given that it's an enormous sheet of manila paper, clumsily dyed in a shade of caput mortuum. He asks, you answer. Yet you might still be in the group obsession, in the collective fantasy of the Gray Studio. Still in that turmoil. He asks, do you answer?

So eventually he'll ask you, *Do you live alone or with your parents?* Then you won't even think, saying to yourself, *I'm thinking nothing,* nor will you feel, saying to yourself, *I feel nothing,* nor will you say anything, anything, saying to yourself, *I'm saying nothing.* Then you'll begin rubbing your hands. Just that. It's enough. Slowly and continuously. As though you were rubbing them to light a fire. Your knees are slightly bent. Your spine in an upright position. As soon as you feel your palms burning, you'll place them behind your back. No need for anything more. You'll massage the area of the supra-renal glands. You'll hold your breath and wait. There are times when a little is a lot. Will the voice asking cease, or will the one who's constantly asking appear? Perhaps, if he does appear, he'll never ask again? Perhaps, if he stops asking, he'll suffer aphony? You have no idea. All you know is that you're continuing to press your back at the same point. You don't know what it is you really want to happen. What for you is less unpleasant or painful. Are you letting your breath flow freely? You think about it. Consider it. Imagine it. You look at your chest. Up and down. Barely perceptibly. Up and down. You hypnotize yourself. Up and down. You eliminate your-self. You swallow. Swallow again. Do you let it go?

The fiction of Michel Faïs leads us into a particularly idiosyncratic area of the self: that of autobiography, which in his case constantly converses with biography. Autobiographical writing, even if fictional, as is the case with Faïs, immediately introduces a fine line between the author-autobiographer and his narrator, as it does not present a single self limited to speaking in the first-person singular. The autobiographical character (whom we encountered as far back as the *Confessions* of Saint Augustine at the end of the fourth century) is from the outset pluralistic, and from this point of view the terms of his self-determination cannot but verge on the borders of illusion. In such a context, every autobiography is related by definition to something or to someone else — even if the correlation is only to emphasize the difference between them. In addition, we should remember that in reconstructing a personal past, autobiography will invariably be connected to the memories and experiences of others, reminding us that the past, however we look at it, constitutes a kind of collective experience. Nevertheless, autobiography basically remains a self-narrative, whose historical recounting fully retains its individual tone, seeking always a core of inner truth. Biography, for its part, is the story of a person recounted by a first-person or third-person narrator, who, even if fictional, as is again the case with Faïs, will include dialogue, characters, and plot, all clamoring to be recorded in the collective background of the person whose biography it is. Nevertheless, biography, too, will keep intact the stronghold of its personal realm, as it has done since at least the late eighteenth century, when it became established as a genre (though it was born in the early post-Byzantine years, drawing on certain elements from antiquity). And this is because, however things developed, what biography will never cease to convey is an intimate picture of its protagonist.

It is precisely on this borderline that the postmodern writing of Faïs moves, operating in an area where the inner truth of autobiography and the intimate picture of biography interact. The novellas *Aegypius monachus* (2001; rev. 2013) and *Lady Cortisol* (2016), which make up the present volume, represent two different yet extremely characteristic phases in the writer's work, from his early and mature periods, revealing the ways in which autobiography and biography come together at the center of it. In order to explain how this takes place, we will have to examine them (obviously not exhaustively) in relation to his other writings published both before and afterward.

Let us look first at the constituents that gave rise to *Aegypius monachus*. Faïs's first work and first novel, *The Autobiography of a Book* (1994), which immediately established him in the Greek literary scene and earned widespread critical acceptance (it should be noted that his work has constantly been the subject of both literary and scholarly criticism from the mid-1990s to the present), is a twofold story: the story of a man that will be transformed into the story of a book or the story of a book that will embrace the story of a man that at the same time will present itself as the story of a birthplace, this being none other than the town in which the author was born: Komotini, in the province of Thrace. In this particular case, the protagonist conceals himself as an aspiring author behind an account of his friend's life, presenting through the latter's narration his own childhood, with that fine line dividing the author-autobiographer from his narrator about which we spoke earlier here under constant threat of dissolution.

In his collection of short stories *From the Same Glass and Other Stories* (1999), Faïs again adopts a form of expression that is introverted and dramatic, combining various forms of discourse within the narrative which he reinforces with a strong element of sarcasm and self-irony, yet he abandons, or so it seems at first sight, the realm of the self. Nevertheless, the personal and autobiographical will return via another door. In place of the one self, doubled or divided, which plays the leading role in *The Autobiography of a Book*, the action is now undertaken by many fallen selves: a world of solitary, alienated, and psychologically or socially frustrated beings as they struggle with their difficult, even paranoia-inducing, fate, living in a state of permanent exile.

And so we arrive at *Aegypius monachus*, in which Faïs returns with all sails unfurled to the self of autobiography, where it appears more openly. The drama of the protagonist, who is identified with the cinereous vulture (its scientific name gives the book its title), is nothing other than his interminable self-deposition, than his unappeased hatred of anything that might idealize him in his own eyes and those of others, than his conviction that he is so enclosed within himself that at any moment he may shrink to nothingness. In *Aegypius monachus*, everything is put to the test, even the therapeutic value of literature, which, though called upon in *The Auto-*

biography of a Book to function to some degree as liberating (in the sense that writing about my sufferings means that I am freed from their burden), is here reduced to flight, to recognized sinfulness, and to inevitable linguistic obtuseness.

Moving forward to *Lady Cortisol*, we find that the pendulum swings once again between autobiography and biography, except that with regard to biography actual characters are refashioned. In his novel *God's Honey and Ashes* (2002), the author wrote of Tzoulio Kaimē (1897–1982), painter, translator, and student of folk culture: a Jewish scholar, in whose Jewish identity Faïs's own Jewish identity—an identity present throughout his works—is mirrored. The self is now disguised as Another and the autobiography has donned the close-fitting garb of biography. With his next novel, *Greek Insomnia* (2004), it is the nineteenth-century poet and prose writer Georgios Vizyinos who is presented; an individual turned completely within himself, buried in the furnace of a self which reveals ever deeper and darker aspects of his inner world, and subject to the one calling that gave rise to insufferable tremors in his life—writing.

The materials that Faïs amasses in his novel *Grave Offerings* (2012) constitute company not only for those in the netherworld but also for those in the world of the living: mnemonic materials that the living will draw from the everyday lives of those who are forever gone. With the crucial difference that these materials, drawn from the life of a family of doctors in the 1960s stigmatized by their Jewish memories, are not pleasant and their value acquires a priori (just as in *Aegypius monachus*) an undeniably negative sign: repugnance for the father's weak character and deep hate (openly erotic) for the mother's departure.

The lonely years of childhood and adolescence in Komotini return once again in Faïs's novel *Out of Nowhere* (2015). The backdrop for all these now very familiar motifs is the psychoanalyst's couch, the basis for *Lady Cortisol*, which immediately followed as the second part of an informal trilogy. A writer and his analyst talk constantly, for months, for years, for an entire decade, without our understanding who is treating whom, without our being able to distinguish the psyche of the therapist from that of the one undergoing therapy. The meetings of the two protagonists are accompanied by short trips across the globe (from New York to Madrid and Manila), where solitary and fearful beings, trapped forever in their egotism (their greatest drama and their only freedom), imitate, sometimes with more, sometimes with less fidelity, the reactions of the psychoanalyst and the one being psychoanalyzed.

The path for the psychoanalytical sessions of *Lady Cortisol* has opened up. Cortisol is the hormone of anxiety and depression, and the woman protagonist in Faïs's monologue is immersed, from the first to the last page, in panic and fear. Perhaps this is why we do not learn her name during the course of the action, while the name Lady Cortisol of the title, which also appears within the text, intensifies the tremulous atmosphere. To what end, however, are the panic and the fear? What is it that makes the heroine twist and turn like a mouse in a trap? From the indications given by the context, the heroine must be sitting rather uncomfortably on the psychoanalyst's couch—though also perhaps not. Obliged to incessantly answer questions put to her by an equally anonymous man, she may feel oppressed by his deliberately neutral voice, though something else may also be happening: she may simply have invented her interlocutor and be using him as a kind of hidden mirror that helps her to bear her frequent crises in an environment characterized by a chilling loneliness and total solitude. In addition, the questions posed to the woman in her tragic monologue are not always those of a therapist (for they are often subject to an underlying paranoia), and, even more, they are never formulated outside her delirium: on the contrary, they constitute parameters incorporated into her own centripetal, compulsive, and unbearably repetitive universe — a universe that, to borrow a line from the poet Nikos Karouzos, endures and suffers from existence, subject to multiple pathologies and the countless voids of existence.

Yet in spite of this, what is the heroine trying to achieve through her answers? Certainly not escape from her fiery circle, which possibly offers her, at least some of the time, a kind of masochistic joy. One of the ways in which we might try to understand her reactions is undoubtedly psychoanalytical. The rules of "acting out" are in force here in every sense of the term: externalize, misbehave, deviate and also act onstage. Onstage Lady Cortisol (in a manner that falls between grotesqueness and unrestrained self-irony) acts herself and her body: her childhood, the guillotine of her family heritage, her fear of death, her sexual appetites (sometimes straightforward emotional loose ends), her prostitution fantasies, and her homosexual inhibitions.

Another way for us to explain the heroine's answers is through the pithy language and narrative. The feverish language in which the heroine is engulfed most probably constitutes the sole reason for her still being alive, the sole reason for her, albeit confined, survival. A similar function is performed by the narrative: by telling stories whose embryonic plots constantly end at the same place, Lady Cortisol attaches no importance to their meaning and aim, concerned only with the pleasure offered by the fetish of recycling them. The author makes use in his novella of techniques he prepared in his previous books: the inner monologue in the third-person singular, lengthy dialogues completely lacking in narrative parts, the incorporation of other voices which multiply the voice of the central narrator—and all this in a text which is spasmodic, with constant twists and repetitions and only a few semblances of plot. Faïs has written a book with a cleverly thought-out architecture and exceptionally powerful internal tensions, very close, as we can easily see, to his previous writings, but at the same time also quite far from them. It is a book that, while seeming to be condemned to present the same tortuous topics, indicates a journey with distinct stages and timely internal shifts: from autobiography to biography and back again—and from there back to a biography that is now transformed into the narration of the life of Others. It is a book that once again will be repeated, the same way and yet entirely differently (as the final part of the informal trilogy), in his last novel to date, *As Never* (2019), introducing again at the center of the narrative psychoanalysis and the lives of Others as projections of the self. Overcome by their angry nihilism, the heroes will reach, willingly or not, the limits of existence, showing that psychoanalysis is but a mask: a mask that wishes to conceal and at the same time to reveal an undeniable emptying, an enormous waste of life that appears not to have a price or any way of overcoming its fiery circle.

Fiction never claims an enviable position in Faïs's writing, which, in place of any fictional plot, prefers the linguistic furnace of both the narrative and the monologues or dialogues that intervene in its unfolding. (This explains the theatrical character of the dialogue parts.) Nevertheless, *As Never* is his least fictional book, if it is at all fictional. Without plot or action, without beginning, middle, or end, without any individual drama (for how might drama be created with a deleted self?), without any fall from a pedestal, without hope, and without expectation of any future, Faïs's creation, shedding light in retrospect on the probable sources of *Lady Cortisol*, recalls Kafka's *Castle*, because of the hero's self-confinement and self-observation, as the critics promptly noted, though I would maintain that it converses more with the theater of Becket. The nightmare is here, and both *Lady Cortisol* and *Aegypius monachus*, whether we note their sources or concentrate on their later reflections, constitute pale (perhaps even black?) farces which will not easily allow us to escape, however we turn, however we react, from their dangerously entwined nets.

Vangelis Hatzivasileiou

MICHEL FAÏS was born in 1957 in Komotini, in northern Greece, and studied economics at the University of Athens. He works as a literary critic, is editor of the books section for the influential Greek newspaper *Efimerida ton Syntakton*, and teaches creative writing at the University of Western Macedonia and at the Open University of Greece. He has published nine works of prose: *Autobiography of a Book* (1994); *From the Same Glass and Other Stories* (1999); *Aegypius monachus* (2001; the revised edition, translated here, was published in 2013); *God's Honey and Ashes* (2002); *Greek Insomnia* (2004); *Purple Laughter* (2010); *Grave Offerings* (2012); *Out of Nowhere* (2015); *Lady Cortisol* (2016); and *As Never* (2019). He was awarded the National Literary Prize in 2000 for his collection of short stories *From the Same Glass and Other Stories*. His books have been translated into English, French, and Romanian, and a number of his short stories have been published in English, French, Spanish, Czech, and Chinese anthologies, as well as in American literary magazines.

He has had two theatrical works staged (*Yellow Dog*, 2009; *Nobody's Bench*, 2014), while several of his books have been adapted for the theater. Together with film director Nikos Panagiotopoulos, he worked on the film scripts for *Delivery* (2004), which was shown at the Venice and Montreal International Film Festivals, *Athens-Constantinople* (2008), and *Rembrandt's Daughter* (2015).

He has held individual photography exhibitions, has taken part in group exhibitions, and has had two photo albums published (*Last Look*, 1996; *City on Its Knees*, 2002).

DAVID CONNOLLY was born in Sheffield, England, and lived all his professional life in Greece before retiring from the Aristotle University of Thessaloniki as Professor of Translation Studies. He has translated over fifty books with works by contemporary Greek authors, and his translations have received awards in Greece, the United Kingdom, and the United States.

Katerina Schina is an essayist, cultural critic, and translator of foreign fiction and poetry. In 1997 she won the translation award in prose from the Greek Literary Translators Association for her translation of Toni Morrison's *The Bluest Eye*, and in 2015 she received the National Book Award in Greece for her essay *Purl Wise*.

Vangelis Hatzivasileiou is a regular contributor to various Greek newspapers and literary magazines. He is the author of *Miltos Sahtouris: The Circumvention of Hyper-realism* (1992), *Road Signs: Orientation Elements in Modern Greek Literature* (2008), and *The Pendulum's Swing: Individual and Society in Contemporary Greek Prose Fiction, 1974–2017* (2018).